I0624867

Books by Tim Hemlin

The Neil Marshall Mystery Series

If Wishes Were Horses . . .
A Whisper of Rage
People In Glass Houses
A Catered Christmas
Dead Man's Broth
Dead Men Don't Pay: A Neil Marshall short story

The Wastelanders Series ~ Science Fiction/Dystopian

The Wastelanders
America Unbalanced: The Wastelanders prequel
Black Silence: A Wastelanders short story

Son of a Kitchen Witch Series ~ YA Urban Fantasy

Son of a Kitchen Witch
The Darkest Night: A Son of a Kitchen Witch novella

Texas Zombie Hunter Blues: A LoneStar short story

Coming Soon ~

The Neil Marshall Mystery Series

Never Give the Devil a Ride

Son of a Kitchen Witch ~ YA Urban Fantasy

The Trickster, Book II in the Son of a Kitchen Witch series

The Wastelander Series ~ Sci-Fi Dystopian

Rise of the Time-Witch, Book II in The Wastelanders series
The Light Maiden: A Wastelanders novella

Visit Tim's Online Bookstore for his buy links

Are you ready for your free story?

Sign up for Tim Hemlin's **newsletter** and receive A Whisper of Rage, A Neil Marshall Mystery story.

Plus, as a subscriber, you will be in the loop for new releases, exclusive deals, updates on upcoming projects and more!

Scan here to subscribe now or visit
http://eepurl.com/bqkPCb

America Unbalanced

The Wastelanders Prequel

Tim Hemlin

America Unbalanced
The Wastelanders Prequel

Copyright © 2017 Tim Hemlin

This book is a work of fiction. The names, characters, places and incidents are products of the writer's imagination or have been used fictitiously and are not to be construed as real. Any resemblance to persons, living or dead, actual events, locale or organizations is entirely coincidental. The publisher does not have any control over and does not assume any responsibility for author or third-party websites or their content.

Published in the United States of America

ISBN: 978-1-945486-07-4

First Edition: May 2017 La Nouvelle Atlantide Press

Cover Art © 2017 by isoga and Bruce Rolff

Cover Design © 2017 by Valerie Hemlin

La Nouvelle Atlantide Press

Dedication

To my grandchildren.

May someday you read this as a curious tale

by your quirky grandfather and not

as a glimpse into your future.

Acknowledgments

Many thanks to my beta readers: Anna Dehennis, faithful supporter since The Wastelanders first came out. Your insightful comments are always appreciated. To James Reid, whose work I greatly admire and whose judgment and critique I highly respect. Despite being in the middle of a move, Bryan Anderson graciously took the time to read and comment on the manuscript. Thanks, my friend, and I look forward to your narration of The Wastelanders. Kudos to Luiz Fernando di Vernieri who went above and beyond the call of duty with a fascinating in-depth commentary. And finally to my compadre and that great writer, Terry M. West, thanks for reading the book and giving me your endorsement. You're awesome.

Special thanks to my publisher, Mike Giusti, who is willing to go to the mat over commas. Every writer should be blessed with a publisher so committed to detail.

And finally, to my readers. I wouldn't be doing this without you. Keep those messages of encouragement coming, and don't be afraid to post a review, or tell your friends. Word of mouth is an author's best friend and greatly appreciated.

Believe me, you keep me going.

You are all, as Bear says, "Marvelous."

Best wishes!

Tim

"To illustrate a principle, you must exaggerate much and you must omit much."

—Walter Bagehot, English Journalist and Economist

Part I

Robin Hood

1

"Whoever said the world won't end with a bang but with a whimper never went through the food riots," the man on the vid declared.

"Ain't that the truth," Holland Copeland echoed as he scrambled a couple of eggs. He turned the flame to low on the antique burner he'd jerry-rigged. His neighbors had thought he was off his rocker when he bought all those canisters of butane and scraped the rust off the old stove out in the storage shed. Lord only knew how long it'd been sitting there and everyone was sure he'd blow himself up. But now who was off their rockers? Power was so inconsistent these days most people ate many a cold meal, if they were lucky enough to get their hands on something to eat to begin with.

"Hunger is the greatest injustice, the utmost betrayal by a government to its people," the candidate continued. "Of course the aristocracy isn't starving. While bread lines become trench warfare and soup kitchens holding stations for well-armed militias; while crops shrivel under the bitter sun and rain fast becomes a myth akin to stories of ancient floods and parting seas, the rich survive on their private stock and personal greenhouses. Trust me. I've seen them."

So does that makes me rich? Holland wondered. He laughed, knowing full well he was poor as dirt. Not a pot to piss in or a window to throw it out of, Deborah had always said. Holland scraped the eggs onto a plate with four pieces of toast and took his food from the kitchen to the living area and sat. The house was small but open, kitchen separated from the dining room table by a wet bar and looking out to the living room which the big screen dominated. Poor as dirt, yessiree. But at least he wasn't hungry.

"Not only do they survive, they grow richer by selling their excess to those who can afford to pay their outrageous price." The man's voice rose. "Outrageous."

Funny, though, how the power always managed to hold when politicians gave what they always called *a major policy* speech. Holland had seen this guy up close, once. He was Senator Leonard Litz and he'd stood taller than Holland had expected, though not quite as tall as Holland or as lanky. But Litz still had the good looks of a film star, not weathered and worn as a fence post like himself.

"So why has the rise of domestic terrorism come as such a shock to the current administration and its supporters?" the voice demanded.

"Amen, brother," Holland agreed. He scooped a fork full of eggs onto a piece of bread and took a big bite. The bread he made himself. He could still get flour at the commissary, and for roughly the outrageous (Litz had that right) cost of two loaves of bread he could make five times that. And he knew there wasn't sawdust or floor scraping stretching out his loaves.

"Terrorists that seemingly strike at will," the man added.

Holland poked his fork toward the vid. "I've been warning the uppers about that for a long time now. Actually, I believe you were one of them, Mr. Senator."

The man went on to say something else but Holland didn't hear because his mobile went off. He muted the big screen. Funny how they always make it look like Litz has these huge crowds listening to him when really it was just vid magic. Well, they might be small but they were fanatical. No doubt about that.

He answered the call with a garbled, "Yeah."

"Captain Copeland?"

Holland swallowed a mouthful of food before responding, "What is it, sergeant?"

"Another food transport's been hit."

"Damn. Where?"

"Out on I-10 near the Barrens."

"Who's out there?"

"Officers Hawke and Clute."

"Tell them to hold tight. I'm on my way."

"Yes, sir."

Holland turned off his mobile. He didn't like staring at people talking to him so he only used the audio. Again people called him a dinosaur but he could care less. Besides, it was probably true.

He shoveled in the rest of his eggs, set the dirty plate on the end table (leaving it there would've driven Deborah crazy) and wrapped the toast in his napkin to eat on the way. Then he strapped on his cutters and lifted his dusty Stetson from the hat rack. The rumbling sound of an old carbon-chewer caught his attention. He cracked open the blinds and peeked outside. Living in an area now considered more rural than suburban usually offered him the privacy he desired. Sure he had neighbors but the closest one was a quarter mile away. Still he got visitors. And usually they were hungry.

Holland had a few chickens and a small hothouse where he grew vegetables. The only reason they prospered was because, being a company man, he had access to affordable water where others didn't. And he had a security system with a generator backup for when the power went offline. No one came in without his approval.

The buzzer rang.

"I see you, Dirk," he said into the speaker.

"It's not Dirk. It's Sara," a woman answered.

"Well, Sara, it's nice of you to pay me a visit but I'm on my way out. I just got called into work."

"Oh." One word but it was said with such a sigh and with so much busted feeling it spoke novels.

"Another time, Sara. And bring Dirk."

"OK, Holland. Thanks." Her voice was barely audible.

Holland turned off the intercom. He straightened his hat, waiting. The truck idled. He peeked out again and saw she had her head on the steering wheel.

"Well, shit," he cussed. He went back into the kitchen. The big screen in the living room still showed the good senator's ranting and raving. He forgot he'd only muted it and clicked the power off. Then he grabbed the half-loaf of bread, started back, changed his mind again and replaced the half with a full loaf. Stepping out the front door of the small ranch house, he waved his hand toward Sara and that ridiculous carbon-chewer she and Dirk still drove. How long did they think their supply of gasoline was going to last them?

"Hang on, Sara," he hollered.

She stopped backing away from the light pulsating blue of the security fence and pulled back in. Her window was already down.

Holland clicked off the fence. "I forgot I still owed Dirk from the poker game last Saturday night. You think a loaf of bread will square us?"

"I reckon that'll square things fine," she replied, wiping her eyes and smiling broadly, the both of them knowing damn well he was lying.

2

"It looks like an inside job," Officer Bernie Hawke stated.

"Why do you say that?" Holland asked. He liked Hawke but for a company man he could be a bit reckless with his words.

Officer Clute, smaller and shorter than Hawke, averted his eyes and wandered over to the wreckage. For partners, they were an odd couple, Holland thought. Beneath Hawke's helmet lay a tuft of thick dark hair and with his weightlifter build he drew a fair amount of attention from the ladies. Randy Clute, on the other hand, was thin and ugly as a ferret who kept his head shaved bald; the man looked like he'd stepped out of a child's nightmare.

"Not many transports come down through the Barrens," Bernie explained, "but it looks like they were waiting for it."

Holland scanned the scene. Lights flashed from the emergency crafts. Signal strobes warned of the crime scene, sealed off to authorized personal only. But out in the middle of nowhere there was hardly a crowd unless you counted the pack of wild dogs in the distance. A man and a woman filmed from all sides. The medical team had made their determination and waited now to finish the job.

"Go on," Holland prodded. The transport was one of the new hovercrafts, supposedly untouchable because of its high-speed capabilities and secure design. It was made from some type of lightweight, ultra-tough and flexible steel alloy stronger than titanium. But there it sat, he noted, in the busted concrete and gravel; a charred shell that's only cargo now consisted of dead bodies.

"Also, it wasn't as heavily guarded as some of the others," Bernie continued. "If I wanted to take down a transport, I couldn't have asked for a better target. It's too tidy for it to be a coincidence. Someone has to be leaking information."

"Points noted," said Holland. In fact, they were good ones. "Not the first time you've proposed this, is it?"

"I don't believe so."

"Be confident, Hawke. It's not."

"Yes, sir. It's not."

"You'd think with the pandemic sweeping Asia there'd be more food around," Clute commented, strolling back into the conversation. Holland wasn't as fond of Clute. Not only was the officer insensitive, he was a racist. On top of that, Clute could barely spit out a thought without worshipping the ground Senator Litz walked on. "Litz is right. We need to keep our food at home and close the borders."

"Right on schedule," Holland said.

Clute's eyebrows furrowed. "Come again, Captain."

"What did you find inside the transport?"

"Driver dead. Three guards, packed to the teeth with weapons, dead."

Holland slipped off his hat and wiped his brow with the back of his hand. Dang sun felt so close these days, like it was vacationing on the moon. "Anything else?" he asked.

"If you mean evidence on who done this," Clute replied, "don't we already know? It was them left-wing radicals."

Holland sighed. "You said it yourself. I need evidence not opinion."

"And by the way," Bernie spoke up, "we don't export as much food as people think."

"Who told you that?" Clute challenged.

"Look it up."

"On what, a government website? Like they're telling the truth."

"Boys, I'm not worried about government websites or our import-export figures. My concern is four dead men and an empty transport." Frankly, Holland thought, the hull looked like a husk Evil had shed before slithering off into the Barrens.

"What do you think they loaded the food in?" Clute asked.

Holland paused. For once the knucklehead raised a good question. He looked west down miles and miles of nothing. Hard to believe this had once been a major artery in and out of the city. But a curious notion came to him as the image of his neighbor, Sara, with her head on that steering wheel lingered in his mind.

He paced around the transport, widening his circle with each completed lap, until his suspicions were confirmed. He knelt on one knee and gently touched a patch of earth, a clear indentation stamped into its dry, clayey surface. "I'll be damned," he muttered.

"Are you thinking they used carbon-chewers?" Bernie Hawke asked.

"Yeah, I find it hard to believe, too." He ran his fingers over the faint tread marks and stood. "But those are tire tracks, all right."

"How far are they going to get down that busted highway?" Bernie asked. He was shading his eyes and peering west.

"Not far," Holland responded, "which is why I think they went east, into the city."

"Then someone had to have seen it, or at least the vids picked it up."

"A reasonable assumption." He turned from the hazy image of the distant skyline to the young officer. "See what you can find out."

"Yes, sir."

"And Hawke, how is that pretty wife of yours?"

"Morning sickness has got her down."

"Yeah, it'll do that. Deborah had an awful time of it." He noticed that Bernie winced at the mention of Deborah's name. These young guys didn't know how to react when he brought her up. "Well, off with you," he ordered, "and let me know as soon as you find something out."

"Yes sir." Officer Hawke wasted no time retreating to his speeder. He climbed on and headed back toward the city. He's a good man, Holland thought. A good man in bad times. Well, maybe that's just what we need.

Clute approached from the backside of the wreckage. "The medical boys want to know if they can bag and haul off the bodies."

"Has the scene been recorded?"

"Yes, sir."

"Tell them to go ahead, then. Oh, and Clute. Have someone take a pic of these tracks. And I want a virtual cast, too."

"What is it?" he asked, skeptically.

"Evidence."

"Whatever you say, sir." As the officer walked off, Holland heard him mutter, "Food in, pandemic out. That's what we need, all right."

God help us, Holland thought, and he went over to his own hovercraft for some water, the back of his throat as dry as the baked earth, a sinking feeling weighing heavy in his gut. As he unscrewed the top of his canteen, he realized it was the same rotten feeling he'd had the day Deborah had announced she was leaving him.

3

"We're going to stick with the game plan," Senator Leonard Litz said. "We're going to do the same things we did in the primaries. Nobody gave us a chance. But we captured the nomination of the Nationalist Party, and we're going to capture the White House."

"What about the conflict of interest accusations?" Mitch Skyler asked.

"Deny them. We're not going to play defense. We're going to keep hammering the administration. We're going to be relentless. We're going to keep telling people how bad things are right now and then how good they're going to be once we take over. We're going to make them want change. We're going to make them want a political revolution."

"The press will call us out," Skyler warned.

They were seated in his conference room. A hard light poured onto the table. A soft glow emanated from a fish tank in the corner. During a break in the conversation, he could hear the water gurgle. Skyler was a good man, Litz thought, but he bowed too often to the winds of caution. He needed to grow a pair. Maybe it'd happen after he lost that baby-faced look and cut that long blond hair.

"The press is on their last leg. GNN doesn't have the guts to come after us. And if they do then we hit back twice as hard. We call them liars. And don't talk to me about the underground press. They're a bunch of leftwing nutcases and we're going to remind people that."

"You're taking a big chance," Skyler said.

"Anytime you take a page from the nationalistic handbook you take a chance," Colonel Rex Fielder spoke up.

Fielder was an interesting character. Military to the bone, he thought he was the reincarnation of George Patton. Like Patton, Fielder was well read, a student of history, and volatile. Litz trusted the colonel to help get him to the top. However, after that it remained to be seen.

"But the advantage we have," Fielder added, "is that the establishment is wounded. People want change. They are literally hungry for it."

"And we're going to keep them hungry," Litz said.

Fielder grinned.

All three men were tall and lean. Fielder, though, appeared the most seasoned. The hardest.

"The problem I see is that we need some support from the establishment we're bashing," Skyler said, "which, I might add, there are those who point out you're a part of, senator."

"According to my esteemed colleagues, I'm hardly a member of the club."

"Regardless, perception is everything and you are a U.S. senator. We're on the high wire and we could use a safety net."

"That's where the governor comes in," Litz pointed out. "Jed Powell is well respected. It's why I picked him as a running mate."

"Being a governor, he's still a D.C. outsider. We need help from the inside."

Litz waved a hand, irritated. "I'm working on it."

Skyler started to object. Litz shot an icy glare and stopped him. "I'm working on it," he repeated. There was a certain congressman with a pretty, young wife he thought a promising prospect for an alliance. A very powerful congressman.

"Allow me to point out the party is falling in line," Fielder interjected. "Whether they've agreed with you in the past is irrelevant. What's important is capitalizing on the enthusiasm. Blind support is always more important than statistics and facts. If the people are enthusiastic, the establishment will follow."

Litz grinned. The man was perhaps more dangerous than he realized. A philosopher and a man of action. Keep him close.

"Well spoken, colonel. President Webster is moving too slowly," he went on. "There are too many regulations mucking up the mag-tech shields. We're going to promise to speed the process. There's no proof that more people will get cancer from the shields than would get it anyway."

"The benefit of the whole is more important than that of the individual," Fielder agreed.

Litz stood and wandered to the window overlooking the sparse city lights. "I recall a time when the night landscape truly was impressive. Lights sparkling." He drew close enough so that the dull interior glow didn't inhibit his view. The country was a mess, and he could fix it. "It will be that way again." He turned back.

"We will continue with our own private logic," the senator told them. "We will force change even if it means deconstructing the United States Constitution."

4

He was known by one name: Bear. Sometimes people attached an article and called him the Bear, as if a distinction needed to be made from others. But there were no others. Bear was, as the saying went, in a class by himself.

If you knew his name, as Hank Mobley did, you fit in one of two categories, enemy or business associate, and often the line between the two blurred. Either way, he had no friends. Or so he claimed. In reality, Bear had so few friends that most everyone believed he hated people, including Mobley.

Mobley considered himself a business associate. In fact, he went out of his way not cross over to enemy. Bear was not a man to tangle with. He was the size of the Texan panhandle and had he a mind to he could guard the Rio Grande alone. Dark as ebony with a bushy black beard and bald head, the last thing you expected to hear when he spoke was the King's English, as Bear had put it. Mobley recalled how shocked he'd been the first time the big man had said something to him. Speechless, in fact. It still surprised him, though at least now he heard the meaning of the words and not just the British accent.

"I come from Shakespeare country," Bear had told him. "You know who Shakespeare was, I assume."

Mobley had shaken his head.

"Oh, pity. I'd always fancied myself akin to Othello, except I treat women better."

At the moment, though, Mobley wasn't thinking of Shakespeare or the King's English or even how a Moorish Brit had made his way to Texas.

Instead he was watching with awe the huge, old carbon-chewer pull into the warehouse. Mobley was scared to death the rumbling would give them away, not to mention the smell of diesel and exhaust, and he didn't breath easy until the engine was turned off and silence slowly filled the large, metallic cavern.

The cab doors opened and out stepped the Bear and two other men.

"Any problems?" Mobley asked as he hit the switch that lowered the large door, sealing off the entrance the truck had driven through.

"Nothing Frick and Frack couldn't blast to smithereens," Bear replied.

"Simon? Crocket?" Mobley prompted. Neither one of them was anything special, a couple of hired guns he could easily replace.

"No witnesses," said the man called Simon.

"I didn't know you were squeamish, Bear," Crocket added.

Mobley drew a sharp breath.

"Gentlemen, I kill when I must."

Their smiles vanished. "I don't think you're as tough as—"

"Shut up, Crocket," Mobley ordered.

"Gunning down soldiers only raises the ire of the army," Bear added. "I've found it makes them more determined to track the perpetrators down."

"We'll be long gone by the time they find the truck," Mobley told him.

"As will I, once I receive my payment."

"The crate of cutters is packed in the hovercraft, just as you requested."

"Marvelous. I hope it doesn't hurt your sensibilities if I inspect the contents."

Mobley nodded toward the hovercraft and they began walking toward it together. Their steps as well as their voices echoed in the vast building. "I'd expect nothing less."

"I should inform you that if your trigger happy lads foolishly believe now's the time to blast me in the back, I've planted a small explosive device on the carbon-chewer. Should I give the signal it's enough to blow up not only the truck but this warehouse and its contents, which of course includes us."

Mobley felt his color drain and he swallowed hard. The man's tone was so pleasant, his face completely deadpan, that it was frightening. "Jesus, Bear."

"It's how we build the trust, mate." Bear opened the crate and looked over the cutters.

Mobley glanced back toward the truck. "Simon, Crocket," he called.

"Yeah," replied Simon.

"Stay where Bear can see you."

"If we'd wanted to cut him down we'd have done it back there," Crocket stated.

Bear raised an eyebrow but continued to focus on the cutters.

"No, I'd be looking for two new hired hands," Mobley said.

Simon laughed. "Whatever."

"Marvelous," Bear said finally, closing the crate. "Pleasure doing business with you." He held a hand out. Mobley met it, big and powerful, and they shook.

"What do you want with all the cutters, Bear?" Crocket asked, moving closer. "You fixing to start a revolution?"

"No, I believe you have your Mr. Litz for that. But if you must know, I have an interested party that very much wants to protect itself once the revolution begins."

"What do you know about Senator Litz?" Mobley asked, his suspicions rising.

"Nothing more than I see in the media."

"He's a good man."

"If you say so."

"There ain't going to be no revolution," Crocket piped up.

"Keep telling yourself that. You might actually believe it by the time it starts."

"There's more where that came from," Mobley told Bear, deciding the big man really didn't know much about Litz.

"There usually is," he replied noncommittal.

"I may be in need of your services again."

Bear showed no emotion. "Call it curiosity, but what do you plan to do with the food?"

Mobley couldn't keep the smile off his face. That cinched it. Bear didn't know. "Let it rot."

"Really? What a pity. There's some prime beef in there, not to mention a plethora of produce."

"Do you want to take any of it with you?" Mobley wondered how he could use it to his advantage. Remember all that beef I gave you? You owe me, Bear. Then he realized the big man was studying him.

"I don't believe I do." Bear climbed into the small hovercraft.

Mobley raised the big door. "Hey, wait," he called, waving his hands. "What about the explosive?"

"Explosive?" responded Bear. "Why would I play with a bloody explosive? A man could get hurt doing that." He raised the craft's window and shot off.

"Sonofabitch," Mobley muttered and let out a short laugh. He had to admit he admired the man. Maybe they could do more business after all.

5

"Bloody hell," Bear muttered. And again. "Bloody hell." Let it rot? They'd killed four men, stolen food from a starving population, and they intended to let it rot. What madness.

He knew he should get himself and the cutters out of the city, but something about this needled his mind and he needed time to think.

Not too far away was a rundown fleabag of a hotel. Bear had seen it in its heyday, when actors, politicians, and generals stayed there. Now if any of them frequented the establishment it was on the sly and by the hour rather than the night.

He left the hovercraft out front and went into the hotel bar. A musty smell met him and the once-plush carpet was so threadbare it looked like a faded tattoo on the saggy arm of an old sailor. Cigarette and cannabis smoke billowed even though smoking in the city was illegal. Bear took a chair at a small round table, intending to sit until he came to a decision. The bartender had other ideas.

"I don't care how big you are," she called. "No one freeloads in here."

"Of course, my dear lady," Bear said amiably. "What do you have that won't strip the lining off my stomach?"

"Oh, a comedian. Well, we don't need no entertainment, neither."

"Do you have anything on draught?"

"Beer."

"Does this beer have a name?"

"St. Arnold."

16

"Ah, the patron saint of Houston. That will be fine."

The bartender, who looked like she'd been rode hard and put up wet a good twenty years ago, poured the beer and put it on the counter. "We don't run no tabs."

Bear smiled and paid cash, adding a handsome tip. "That hardly surprises me."

The woman, seeing the extra money, softened some. "Maybe, I could make an exception for you."

He nodded slightly. "I'll keep that in mind." Bear sat back down with his beer and took a swig. For an American brew, St. Arnold's was rather good.

There was no music in the sad little bar, only the muttering of voices and the repeated scenes of the food riots on the big screen above the bar. Miami, the Los Angeles peninsula, Chicago, hungry people took to the streets, breaking store windows, setting fires, and clashing with police in riot gear. Closer to home, San Antonio and Austin were in unrest, and Houston was ready to burst at any moment. Bear felt it. He took another drink of beer, telling himself he needed to let it all go and get out.

And then from the corner of his eye, he spotted her. Even before she struck up a conversation, and against his better judgment, Bear knew what he was going to do.

The girl's black skirt was so short it barely covered her. Bear had worn bandannas made of more material. Black fishnet stockings stretched up her lean legs and the spiky heels of her shoes added a couple of inches to her diminutive frame. Her sleeveless top, also black, exposed her flat stomach, and hugged her ample bosom. Dark hair cropped short, pouty lips and large brown eyes, she was the type of girl high school boys drooled over and old men now paid handsomely for in order to experience the privilege they never had in their youth. Frankly, the sight of her only added to Bear's depression.

"You looking for a party?" the girl asked, taking the chair opposite him. "Though you are kind of big. Maybe I should get insurance first."

"Simply drinking a lager, love."

She sighed. "A girl's got to eat."

"The food any good here?"

"Dreadful." She gave a short shrug, hands out. "But it's better than starving."

Bear faced the haggard bartender. "Two more of these," he ordered, pointing at the mug, "and what's the daily special?"

She eyed him like he'd lost his mind. "Daily special? Sure, we got a daily special. We got jerky, pickled eggs and crusty bread. And since it's a feast fit for a king, it costs a king's ransom."

Maybe I should've taken some of that food left to rot after all, he told himself. "Marvelous. Two plates."

Turning back, he whispered to the girl, "What kind of jerky?"

"You don't want to know."

"Ah."

"But for food I'll give you all afternoon."

Bear drank more beer before responding. "It is tempting, my love. However, should we someday meet again, I suspect it would be under very different circumstances and I wouldn't want you to be embarrassed."

The girl stared at him as if he'd spoken in Swahili. "You're a strange man. What's your name?"

"Bear."

"Yeah, most men don't use their real names here."

"Believe what you wish, but my real name is Bear. What's yours?"

"Rachel."

Yes, of course, he thought. Rachel. Again he glanced at the screen and its continuous stream on the food riots live on GNN, the Government News Network. Someday, he thought, that may well be the only news outlet left and should a soul want the complete truth he'll have to seek out underground sources. How did the old poet put it? The times they are a-changing. And in this case, not for the better.

"Well, Rachel my lovely, I have a proposition for you."

"Food's up," the bartender called as if Bear was the waiter.

Rachel eyed him warily. "Can I eat first?" She jumped up, willing to retrieve the plates the bartender had set out.

"Absolutely, my dear. And then you're going to help me distribute real food to a lot of hungry people."

6

Senator Leonard Litz cut into a thick round of beef. Grilled crisp on the outside, rare in the middle, the knife slid right through it. Sides of rosemary new potatoes and asparagus with lemon butter accompanied the main course.

"Tenderloin," his dinner companion heard him say as he displayed a juicy piece of the meat on the tip of his fork, "prepared properly will melt in your mouth." Right on cue he put the bite between his lips and chewed slowly. Then he jabbed the empty fork in the air and after swallowing added, "However, if overdone even tenderloin becomes tough and unappetizing. Governor Powell, my running mate, is fond of pointing that out."

Sitting across from him, Isabelle Bishop dabbed her lips with a napkin. She still didn't know why he'd asked her here, but one thing she'd learned as a young newcomer to the Emerald City was patience. Technically they weren't in D.C. but New York at a posh restaurant atop a Manhattan high-rise, the building owned, she knew, by a wealthy Litz supporter. Floor to ceiling windows surrounded the space, and every so often she caught a reflection of herself, young and lean, her dark Latino features alluring to most of the men she encountered. Outside it was night and amazingly few other lights in the city were on. Inside, soft lighting highlighted the attractiveness of the couple; she knew they looked good together. A pianist provided background music.

"Oh?" she replied at last. Yes, technically New York, but it was a D.C. power meeting.

Litz took a small drink of his wine, a French Cabernet. "It's the same with civil unrest. We need to maintain that sweet spot where people are hungry." He paused, grinning, "And I mean that literally. Hungry and wanting change but not so desperate they start forming their own militias and create city-states. Reigning them back in would be unnecessarily tough at that point."

She took a very small taste of wine and again waited. It was obvious he enjoyed her company and was entertaining her. She also knew he was entertaining his ego just as much, if not more. Absent, though, were the famous Litz rants. Calm and cultured, he projected an image much different than the one seen in public.

"Yes," he continued, "I can see it on your face. Why did the senator invite me to dinner, alone, without my husband?"

A subtle lift of her eyebrows up and down silently responded *why, indeed?*

"My dear Isabelle, are you not hungry?" he asked.

"My appetite comes and goes these days," she replied. Absently she touched the diamond pendant around her neck as if afraid it had disappeared, stories of brazen robberies having breeched even the most protected enclaves. Betraying her fear, though, embarrassed her and prompted the tiniest sip of wine. A taste on the tip of her tongue not because she disliked wine. In fact, she appreciated a fine vintage, and this was very good. However, she wanted to keep her senses. Attracted to a man outside her marriage was bad enough, which was why she wore the conservative black evening dress with the high collar. Attracted to possibly the next president was worse.

Litz nodded politely and ate another bite of tenderloin. "Well, let me put my cards on the table," he said. "I asked you to dinner because I need your help."

"My help? But my husband is the chairman of the House Ways and Means Committee, not me." She recognized the irony. For all his talk, Litz needed an in with the very establishment he constantly berated and that had tried to marginalize him over and again.

"Precisely."

"J. Henry Bishop is his own man," she told him through a practiced smile.

"I have no doubt. However, I'd be a fool not to see that an intelligent beauty such as yourself has influence over her husband."

Wisely, she thought, he'd added intelligent and didn't leave beauty hanging out there by its lonely superficial self. "Thank you." She cut a piece of the tenderloin and tasted it. In spite of herself, her face lit up.

The smugness Litz emanated made her want to stab him in the hand with her fork.

"Once again, I believe it's my husband you should be entertaining."

"I fully intend to."

Isabelle started to lift her wine then caught herself. "I'm afraid I'm still learning my way around," she told him, "but it seems to me you've only put half your cards on the table."

A chuckle escaped Litz. "False modesty does not become you, my dear. From what I've observed you're a fast learner, a fast learner indeed. You're stepping into the role of a politician's wife quite well." He finished his tenderloin, left the potatoes untouched, and ate just the tips of the asparagus. Then he set his fork and knife on his plate and laced his fingers together with his elbows resting on the table. "If I may be frank?"

"Please do."

"J. Henry wields more power than he realizes. The southwest desalination project has stalled—the money dried up. We can't afford any more delays. A word of support from him would go a long way to reviving it."

"What I think you mean is that you'd like him to derail the calls to form a select committee to investigate the misappropriation of funds. Am I right?"

"As I said, a fast learner." He waved a hand. "The corruption charges are politically motivated, put forth by shortsighted fools."

"So all this talk of creating a Water Cartel isn't true?" she asked.

A wince creased the corners of his eyes and weakened his political smile. It was as if he'd heard her tail rattling. "Who's to know what will happen once all the desalination projects are up and running? Look at how well they're working here on the east coast. Boston and New York would've sunk like Atlantis without them."

"Parts of the cities now have floating buildings," she pointed out.

"Adds the charm of old Venice."

Isabelle sliced off another sliver of meat and slowly ate it. "J. Henry will be putting his neck on the chopping block," she said.

"A deed that will not go unrewarded."

"If the axe doesn't fall, you mean."

"Great remunerations require the willingness to take great chances."

Isabelle ate another piece of meat and this time chased it with a mouthful of wine. "You will need to speak with J. Henry," she reiterated.

"Absolutely. And when I do, will I have his wife's support?"

Isabelle broke into a beautiful smile. "Let's talk about these remunerations."

7

Bear knew they wouldn't expect to see him again, or at least not so soon. After he'd left the young lady of the streets, fairly confident she'd follow through on his instructions, he briefly considered recruiting a couple of hired guns. After all, Bear had a crate of cutters at his disposal and unemployed manpower lingered at every corner. But desperate times made desperate men, eroding Bear's trust in humanity. He didn't need anyone turning on him once the bounty was in hand. He didn't want to kill any more than necessary.

The warehouse had surveillance vids, which were easy enough to scramble. They were old-style on a common frequency meant to keep out riffraff, never imagining that a more sophisticated threat would ever desire entrance. Bear set the scramblers and waited near a rancid smelling dumpster, no one else in sight. It was possible one of Mobley's thugs would come out and check the stream, making his work so much easier.

The sun was brutal against the shade-less, broken concrete. It was like cinder blocks of heat were falling on his shoulders and neck. A lifetime ago he'd lived for a short time in Mumbai and it had been the hottest place he'd ever known. Now the rest of the world seemed to be catching up.

Bear had the patience of a snail but time in the heat passed very slowly and he began to contemplate moving on to Plan B. However, Plan B was messy, loud and likely to attract unwanted attention. He waited a little longer.

Finally the side door adjacent to the truck door opened. Simon stepped outside, cutter in hand, followed closely by Crocket. Bear hunkered down, out of sight. They circled left and right, the harsh sun reflecting off their dark glasses, until they stopped at the top of the loading zone. Satisfied they were alone, they then turned their backs to Bear, and Simon, shading his eyes, looked up at the mounted vids. He pointed at them with his cutter and said something that from his distance was unintelligible. Crocket nodded his head in agreement, and Bear knew this was his chance.

For a big man, he had a light, quick step. He was within feet before the men heard him and turned back around. "What do you want?" Crocket demanded.

Bear shot Simon first, since he had yet to put his cutter away. The surprise on Simon's face matched Crocket's expression as the other thug tried too late to reach for his cutter. Bear squeezed a pair of blasts into Crocket.

"I told you I kill when I must," he said and left both bodies on the busted pavement.

Bear went through the door the men had left open. A swath of the inside lights had been turned off, though a few illuminated the hulking carbon-chewer as another man along with Mobley inspected its contents. It looked to Bear like they were gutting a dragon, pleasing themselves before leaving the rest to perish.

Cutter in hand, Bear calmly crossed over to them.

"I'm just telling you it's a shame," Mobley was saying.

"That's the way he wants it," the other man replied, slightly exasperated. They stood just inside the back doors of the rig, staring in at its contents. From the unknown man's tone they'd obviously gone over this already. "He intends to incite the masses, rile them up."

"Well, this ought to do it. But they won't miss a few pounds of beef or a bushel of apples or a sack of potatoes."

"You better hope he doesn't find out. He'll skin you alive."

"The only way he'll find out is if you tell him." Mobley swung around to face the man as he said this, and that was when he saw Bear. "You forget something?" he asked, more confused than alarmed until he spotted the cutter in the big man's hand.

"Actually, I did," Bear responded. "Out of there."

The other man looked to see the source of Mobley's concern. He was lean and wore army fatigues. He had a wolfish jaw and eyes just as cold and unimpressed at the weapon aimed at them. "Who are you?"

Mobley answered for the big man. "He masterminded the hijacking. Carried it out perfectly, for that matter."

"You talk too much," the man in the fatigues said.

Mobley paled.

"Well, what are your intentions?" the military man asked Bear.

"Redistribution."

An amused smile touched the man's face. "You can't be serious."

"I killed two men already. I don't have a problem killing two more. Really, the choice is yours." For a split second Bear wondered if he should even be giving them a choice. After all, he hadn't offered Crocket or Simon that courtesy. Then a slight glance upward gave the man in the fatigues away, and Bear knew there was someone else with them.

Bear ducked a split second before a blast came his way. In a crouch, he pivoted and fired toward its source. The blasts grazed the bottom of a catwalk. Bear saw a man recoil, and he fired again, hitting him. The man tumbled off the catwalk and down.

While Bear was engaged with the guard, the man in the fatigues had shoved Mobley off the end of the trailer and jumped. The big man stumbled as Mobley fell into him.

From his knees, a terrified Mobley stared at Bear. Bear cracked him over the head with the butt of the cutter and Mobley collapsed. He searched for the man in the fatigues and caught a flash of green as he disappeared out the door. Bear fired even though he knew it was too late.

Bear hurried to the door. A glint in the searing sunlight instinctively caused him to duck, and a pair of blasts ricocheted off the door frame. He pulled back, counted to three in his head, then rolled into a crouch, cutter aimed at the spot where he'd seen the glint and let loose a couple of blasts. The man, however, had put a fair amount of distance between them. Bear stood and watched. Curiously, the man's gait was awkward, a little stiff like he'd pulled a muscle, though his pace proved respectable enough Bear knew he'd not catch him. He hoped he'd not made a mistake by not shooting the man on sight.

Back inside the warehouse, he raised the big door. If Rachel had done her job, company should be arriving soon. He pulled the poor bastard who'd fallen from the catwalk along with Simon and Crocket's bodies to the back of the warehouse, out of sight. Mobley tempted him but Bear simply couldn't execute the man. Besides, he was moaning.

Locating a good old-fashion roll of duct tape, Bear slapped a strip on the moaning man's mouth then bound his hands and legs. He picked him up like he was nothing more than a sack of onions and carried him up a flight of iron stairs to an office. After kicking the door open, Bear dropped Mobley on the floor. He planned to tip off the cops on the whereabouts of a few of corpses after he left. Why he didn't add this one to the list he couldn't say. It just didn't feel right. So Bear leaned down and said calmly into Mobley's ear, "I know you can hear me. I know you're not hurt as severely as you pretend. If you tell the authorities I was here, I'll return and finish the job." And he walked out.

Again Bear wondered about the military man with Mobley. He had to know that soldiers had died in the hijacking. Yet that didn't appear to bother him any more than having a cutter pointed at his head. Nerves of steel, a heart of ice; a man who believed in causes more than humanity. That alone made him very dangerous. *He intends to incite the masses, rile them up.* So what was his cause? And who was the rogue in fatigues talking about?

8

The gurgle of an old model transport broke Bear's thoughts. It swept the area, a circumspect approach ready to reverse its progress at the first sign of trouble. Bear stood at the top of the loading zone, just outside the shade of the building, and waved an arm. Slowly the transport edged closer. Tired old thing, he thought, didn't have many useful years left. Then again, how many of us did?

The transport stopped outside the warehouse. It was the type the postal service had used years back when people still had money to spend on gifts and items they didn't really need but just had to have. The doors raised and three men climbed out along with Rachel. The driver was a young Hispanic kid, very nervous. From the passenger's side a middle-aged man emerged, average height with thinning hair and the thick hands of someone who'd done his share of labor, but he wore the collar of the old religion. The third man was near the driver's age and anxious temperament.

"Hello Father Bartholomew," greeted Bear.

"Ah, so it is you," the priest responded. "The girl claimed you were here, but honestly I didn't believe her."

"Ye of little faith."

He shook a finger at the big man. "Not yet, Bear. I haven't reached that point yet." As he approached, he said, "This is Carlos and his friend Gabe."

Bear shook their hands. Carlos was the driver.

"Carlos works at the church," the priest added. "Carlos, this is Bear, the man I've told you about."

"What lies have you been perpetuating, Bartholomew?" Rather than shake hands, the two men embraced and then moved into the shade of the warehouse followed by the young Hispanics and the lady of the streets.

"Not lies," the priest countered. "Hope."

"Perhaps, then, this is your lucky day. Do you still distribute food to the poor?"

"Not as much as we used to, I'm afraid. Only on days when we're fortunate enough to get our hands on stale bread and half-rotten vegetables and fruit."

"Well, there's nothing rotten about this," Bear told the priest, leading him to the carbon-chewer. "I saw to that."

Bartholomew's eyes widened as he absorbed the bounty of the trailer. "How did you come by this?"

"Let's just say some disagreeable lads had planned to let it turn rank."

"I wish I could believe you, Bear."

"With God as my witness, I speak the truth."

Rachel, Carlos and Gabe climbed into the trailer. "This is real food," she said, astonished.

"It'll go bad quickly in this hot warehouse," Bear told them. "You need to get it into hungry bellies soon."

"That will hardly be a problem," the priest said.

Bear returned to the big door, took a good look at the transport and decided it would work. Then he scanned the horizon, remembering the soldier awkwardly retreating. "We'd do well to move with haste," he announced. "Carlos, pull your rig as close to the carbon-chewer as you can."

Bartholomew agreed and with the help of Rachel and the Hispanics, they transferred the food to the transport. After Carlos backed it out, Bear lowered the big door and deactivated his scramblers. Poor Mobley would have to wait a little longer.

"Why are you just giving this away?" Rachel asked Bear. She rode with him to the church. They followed the clunky transport, its back end low to the ground from its cargo.

"My plan had never been to take it for myself," he answered.

"But now you have it."

"No, the good father has it."

"You could make a pretty penny," she chimed, her voice rising.

"When opportunity knocks, I'm not above opening the door. However, there are times when personal satisfaction supersedes economics."

"I thought economics feeds personal satisfaction. Literally."

"On occasion," he admitted. "But at this point I'd rather feed others."

"You won't take any of it?" she asked.

Bear winked. "I wouldn't go that far, love."

"Well, I'm going to get my share and get out," she told him. "And if you're smart, you'll do the same. Once word of this hits the streets it's going to be chaos."

And it was.

Young and old descended on the dilapidated church like Santa Anna's army on the Alamo. They filled what had once been a parking lot but was now a field of cracked pavement dotted by makeshift tents of the dispossessed and stumps of long dead live oak trees. Bear had intended to heed the girl's advice, take enough food to sustain him for a few days and leave. But with the swelling crowd he felt obligated to help keep order. Father Bartholomew abhorred attention and grew frightened and disoriented at the pushing and shoving, and then the press appeared, the investigative reporters demanding to know where he'd gotten the food. By then the activity had also drawn the attention of the police, and Bear quietly slipped into the musty rectory, within earshot to keep tabs of what was going on but out of sight.

"It was donated by anonymous," the priest responded over and over again. "That's all I know. Anonymous."

To placate the officers, Bartholomew offered them a portion. In return, they kept order until finally the last of the food was dispersed and the crowd thinned.

The press stopped its live streaming and started packing up as well. One of the remaining reporters approached Bartholomew. "Off the record," she said, "who's behind this?"

The priest opened his arms, palms up. "I can only say the patron wishes to remain—"

"I know," she cut in, "anonymous. Saint Anonymous."

"Or Robin Hood," one of the officers muttered, holding his own rewards as he left.

A spark came to the reporter's eyes. "Robin Hood," she muttered. "Hmm."

Father Bartholomew forced a smile before joining Bear, Carlos and Gabe inside the rectory. "Some people are calling you a saint," he told the big man. "Others say Robin Hood. What say you?"

"Bah. A bunch of humbug, the both."

"Saint Robin works for me today," the priest told him. "Join me in a

28

glass of sacramental wine, my friend, and spend the night. I would very much enjoy an evening of lively conversation, perhaps talk a little treason."

"Tempting as it is, I must go. I have obligations. And I fear I pushed my luck as far as I dare."

"I understand. I can't say I like it, but I understand. However, before you leave there's something I must tell you." He glanced at Carlos and Gabe who were slouched in chairs, exhausted. Bartholomew nodded his head and Bear followed.

"Marvelous the way you handled the authorities," he said.

"One foot in this corrupt world with the other feeling for ground in a better one, Bear." The priest led Bear into the kitchen and flicked on a light. At that moment, power went down and Bartholomew had to locate an electric torch.

"What troubles you, my friend?" Bear asked.

"Much." He took a deep breath and said, "I dreamt about you the other night. Normally, of course, I keep my dreams to myself. But as you have better sight than I," he let his voice trail off.

"Dream you say? Of me?" Bear's crossed his arms and leaned against a counter. It could be nothing. Then again. . . .

"We were in a desolate area, earth cracked, scorching sun drying up the very soul of life as we know it. Yes, I was with you. Along with Carlos and Gabe and many others. It was like an old wagon train, only there were no horses. Just a hawk spiraling above us. I tried to point it out to you but you said, 'Hold tight, mate, it won't be long now. Soon we'll come to water. And trees. And that is where you'll make your new beginning.'" The priest stopped. His hands were shaking.

Bear uncrossed his arms and stood straight. "Is this really a dream, padre? Or are you trying to tell me something?"

"I dreamt of you, Bear, and of a hawk following you as you crossed a barren land. And I placed myself in the dream. Do you understand what I'm saying?"

"No," he replied. "Surely you don't want to live in emptiness."

Bartholomew cracked a smile. "If it's good enough for the Buddhists, it's good enough for me."

"Be serious. My time is short." It came out curter than he'd intended, but he was feeling the ticks of time like taps of a cutter barrel against his back.

"I am serious. Emptiness, barrenness, desolation; that's what the inner city has become. People are hungry, frightened, and angry. You can feel it in the air. It's going to get worse before it gets better. And mark my words; the better will not be good. I smell the sulfur of Satan, Bear. Evil preaches and people are listening. The fabric of society is tearing apart and the stitches of hate simply allow it to bleed to death. There will be no mending in this climate." Bartholomew drew a sharp breath and clutched his heart as he sank back against the sink.

"Father, are you OK?"

"There, I said it. I got it out."

"I can't take you with me."

"Then we will die."

"Don't speak like a fool." Bear turned and left the kitchen. He wasn't responsible for Father Bartholomew or any of them. After all, hadn't he already given them more than anyone else in months? Perhaps years? The ungrateful sot.

He grabbed the modest sack of vegetables and meat he'd set aside and walked out of the rectory. He'd left his hovercraft inside the fenced compound on the opposite side of where the throngs had been. The city's blackout allowed a shaving of stars to be visible against the gunmetal sky. Bear hated the city and vowed never to return. As he fired up the hovercraft and lifted it over the fence, he used a disposable mobile to put in a call to the police. Mobley, the poor bastard, had probably pissed his pants by now.

9

"Senator Litz, explain what you meant when you recently said the day of the pope is over."

"I didn't say that."

"You did, sir, at a rally in Manchester, New Hampshire."

"No, that's not exactly what I said."

"Maybe you can clarify your statement, then. It's left many in the country confused."

"There's nothing confusing about it. The time has come to cut ties with imperial Rome. While the pope sits in his palace, we have people starving in the streets. Then he has the nerve to criticize me for wanting to keep our country safe."

"Are you talking about your proposal to close our borders to the world?"

"I'm talking about keeping America safe. Pandemic stays out, food stays in."

"Senator—"

"Sorry, I'm late for a meeting."

10

Officer Bernie Hawke had tracked the illicit carbon-chewer to the warehouse district. The anonymous tip to the police department simply expedited his search. He wondered why someone would bother to call in a tip, especially once he entered the building with half a dozen other officers and found the dead men. Most people would simply let the putrid smell of decay be the calling card.

With the exception of some bruised apples, lettuce scraps, and other such minor leafy debris, the trailer was empty. Bernie looked at the dead men as the forensic team began their job of documenting the scene. The corpses appeared to be hired guns, though obviously not very good ones.

Bernie called Captain Copeland. "I found it," he said.

"And?"

"Empty."

"Not surprising. I heard a local church had a big food giveaway today," Holland said. "You think there's a connection?"

Bernie knew the man was being sarcastic. "I think something went wrong. There are three dead men here."

"I'm sure they were upstanding citizens. Regardless, we need to find out who did this, Robin Hood or not."

"Sir?"

"That's what the press is calling him. Or her. Steal from the black market rich and give to the food deprived poor. Will someone say hallelujah?"

"What do you want me to do?" Bernie asked.

"Find out what you can then go home to that pretty wife of yours. We'll talk in the morning."

"Yes sir." As Bernie disconnected, he mumbled, "Hallelujah."

"We got a live one," someone called.

Bernie turned from the entrance to the warehouse and hustled inside. One of the other cops was leading a man down a flight of stairs. The man was rubbing his wrists. He was pale, shaky, and had wet himself.

"Who's this?" Bernie asked.

"Name's Hank Mobley. Found him in the office."

"Well, Mr. Hank Mobley, it appears you're lucky to be alive. Why?"

"I don't know," Mobley replied.

"Of course you don't." Bernie pointed to the trailer. "What do you know about this ancient piece of crap?"

"Nothing."

"Did you know those three men?"

"No."

"Do you know anything?" Bernie pushed. "Let's start with why you're here because I think you know exactly what happened."

A man behind him cleared his throat. "That's enough, officer."

Bernie turned and spotted a man in plain clothes. "Who are you?"

"Lieutenant Lewis Walsh," he replied. "This is my investigation now." He nodded and the man with Mobley led him away.

"Captain Copeland is very interested in this case," Bernie said.

"Copeland, huh?" The man might just as well have said horse piss instead of the captain's name. "So you're with Special Forces. Well, well, well, why is SF interested in an empty artifact?"

"A transport of food was hijacked in the Barrens and this empty artifact carried the cargo off after leaving four dead men. Add the three in this warehouse, and it was an expensive haul."

Walsh was a short, stalky man with a ruddy face and corruption written across his dark uni-brow. "So this is where the food came from," he muttered. "I'm going to need to have a talk with that priest, only he's going to be the one confessing to me."

"Don't you find it odd three men are dead yet one's alive and kicking?"

"If he knows anything, we'll get it out of him. Could be the poor bastard was just in the wrong place at the wrong time."

Or at the right place with the right cop, he thought. "So Robin Hood left a witness?" Bernie asked.

"Who the hell's Robin Hood?"

Bernie assumed Walsh wasn't asking about the legend, though he had his doubts about the man's intellectual depth. Nonetheless, he responded, "That's what the press is calling whoever gave the food to the church."

"More reason to have a conversation with Friar Tuck."

OK, he knew the legend. "You think he'll know?"

"Oh, they always know, Mr. Special Forces Officer."

"I think the guy you just hauled off is going to know more."

Walsh shrugged his shoulders. "Who's to say?"

"My report will go to Captain Copeland," Bernie stated.

Walsh hardened. "Are you threatening me?"

"No sir," Bernie replied. "I'm only doing my job."

"What's your name, boy?"

In the past Bernie might've winced. Now he calmly said, "Officer Bernard Hawke."

"Well, Officer Bernard Hawke, I won't forget you."

"Nor I you. Sir."

11

Bernie Hawke was exhausted by the time he made it home. Home was an apartment on the southwest side of the city. They couldn't afford a house yet.

He hiked up a flight of stairs and hit the remote lock. When nothing happened he knew the power was out again. He used his key and went inside.

It was late. A single candle burned on the stove top. Bernie unloaded his gear and left it near the entrance. Late as it was, he figured Kelly was asleep. She wasn't.

"Hi," she said drowsily as she sat up on the couch. An old afghan that had been often repaired and passed down through the family slid to her waist. Her dark hair was a little mussed, but her blue eyes sparkled at the sight of him. That look always sent a shock of shivers through him.

"What are you still doing up? I thought you had court tomorrow."

"I do. I couldn't sleep." She stood. "Are you OK?"

"I'm fine."

"I heard about he food riot in town at Sacred Heart—"

"It wasn't a food riot," he interrupted.

"Then Robin Hood is true?"

He smiled. "You snarky little thing. You knew there wasn't a food riot."

"I don't trust anything from the central media these days. And when the power goes down, the underground sources do too."

"Then how did you know about Robin Hood?"

"It's all over the media, stupid," she replied. "Both what the government still calls media and the underground. At least before the power died."

Bernie sat down and put his arms around her. "I love you dearly, but you're going to get me in trouble."

"Probably," she muttered, snuggling into him.

He laughed in spite of himself. "Have you eaten?"

"I had some broth."

He touched her belly. "That's not enough."

"Excuse me, but I'm giving birth to a warrior," she joked. "He needs to learn to tough it from the get-go."

"Oh, you are a hard ass."

"Now you know that's not true." They kissed and she patted him on the chest. "Have you eaten?"

"I'm not hungry." He got up and walked toward the kitchen.

"Liar."

Bernie grabbed a beer from the dark fridge. It was still cold enough. He popped the top off and drank.

"Where'd the food come from?" she asked.

"A hijacked transport." He took another pull from the beer and raised his hand. "But before you say Robin Hood again," he added, "I don't think that was the intent. The scene reeks of a deal gone bad. There were three dead men in the warehouse and one live one who'd been bound. If you're going to kill three, why leave one alive? A witness."

"Because you know him," Kelly answered. "Maybe not a friend but a contact. Someone you've done business with before and might again."

Bernie nodded as he drank. "Exactly."

She tapped the seat next to her and he sat back down. "What did this witness have to say?"

"Nothing. As soon as I started questioning him, an unpleasant cop named Lieutenant Walsh came in and swooped him away. Know him?"

"I don't. You think it was a coincidence?"

"No."

"You think he's dirty?"

Bernie finished his beer. "It wouldn't surprise me. I'll put Walsh on Holland's radar, if he's not already there." He sighed. She leaned against his shoulder. "What about you?" he asked. "You ready for tomorrow?"

It was Kelly's turn to sigh. "It doesn't look good, Bernie. It doesn't look good at all. If the judge doesn't give us a temporary stay, you'll start seeing surveillance vids go up all over the city. And once up, they won't come down." She sat straighter. "You know how I used to say our civil rights are being chipped away little by little? Well, they're not being chipped at, anymore. We're handing them over freely. Privacy? Who needs it? Pretty soon the only privacy we're going to have is the privacy the government allows. Thank you, Senator Litz, for the Surveillance Act.

"Did you know," she went on, "he has ties to the company monitoring the vids? He gets elected, it'll be the most corrupt administration since the early Twenty First Century."

"You get yourself all worked up, you'll never sleep tonight."

"Ha, like that was a possibility to begin with. Besides, you probably like the Sur Act. If Litz could've pushed it through sooner you'd know the identity of Robin Hood."

"They had vids at the warehouse," Bernie told her. "But they recorded nothing but static."

"That's weird."

"Not so." He rose and wandered back into the kitchen.

"What aren't you telling me?"

"Technology, my dear. It's why I don't think the Sur Act is anything more than political lip service. There's a new technology floating around out there called scramblers. I think our Robin Hood had his or her hands on it. So the next step for the Sur Act enthusiasts is to develop scrambler blockers. It's a cat and mouse game, Kel, cat and mouse."

"No, Bernie, it's more than that. If anything, the government's the cat and our civil liberties are hanging from its mouth with only the tail showing."

Bernie popped open another beer. "Then I guess you'd better win tomorrow," he said, and drank.

"Sure, put it all on me."

"I have faith."

"I'm glad someone does." And her smile faded.

12

"Lew Walsh," Captain Holland Copeland repeated. He tipped his head back and looked up as if apologizing to God for blasphemy. "And you say he took the witness away?"

"One of his men did, yes," Bernie replied.

"Wonderful."

They were downtown in Holland's office. On the wall above a bookcase hung a large framed picture of his graduating class at the academy. A few smaller stills surrounded it, including one of Holland shaking hands with the mayor and another of him making a touchdown catch back in high school. He'd been a tight end. A couple of filing cabinets had unfiled folders stacked on top. On his desk he still kept a picture of Deborah.

"I take it you know him?" Bernie asked.

Holland made a beeline for the academy picture and tapped the image of a dark, swarthy man in the second row with his hands behind his back. "He was a weasel then and time's only made him more weaselly." He faced Bernie. "But he's not stupid. He's always managed to keep his head above the sewage he treads in. Be careful around him, Bernie."

"I don't figure we'll be crossing paths too often."

"Then you figured wrong." Holland grabbed his Stetson from the hat hook on the back of his door. Everyone in the department knew not to throw his door open too wide. God help the man who crushed his crown. "Come on," he said.

"Where we going?" Bernie asked.

"The Montrose precinct to track down Walsh. I want a word with the witness."

Bernie drove the unmarked hovercraft. Despite Holland's warning, he wasn't afraid of Walsh. He'd dealt with blowhards before. However, he was worried about Kelly. The stress of the case had gotten to her. And her normal optimism was fading.

"Pull in here," Holland said, tugging Bernie back to the job at hand. "Right in front."

"Yes, sir." Bernie eased the craft to a stop parallel to the entryway. It wasn't a parking spot, but the captain was making it one. They passed from the raging heat to clammy comfort of the inside the building. Power must've been out and just come back on, Bernie thought. Even when the generator took over, it never cooled the building. At the inner door they each gazed into the iris recorder and the lock sprung open. Halfway down the hall, Holland veered left and entered a cluster of cubicles. Bernie followed, stopping when the captain did.

Lew Walsh locked his hands behind his neck and leaned back in his chair. "Well, what took you so long, captain?"

"I want to talk to Mobley."

"That's a fine how-do-you-do from an old classmate." Walsh's gaze trailed to Bernie. "Good morning, Officer Hawke."

"Where's Mobley, Lew?" Holland demanded.

"Released. We had no reason to hold him."

"What'd you find out?"

"Nothing. Someone ambushed them. Killed the guns and jumped Mobley from behind."

A crooked smile distorted Holland's face. "And you believe that?"

Walsh swung the chair forward, his elbows landing on the desk. "Hell, no. But he's more afraid of whoever done it than he is of us."

Holland flattened his hands on the lieutenant's desk and leaned down. "I find that very hard to believe, Lew."

Walsh didn't flinch. "Believe it, Holland."

"I want to see his file and the transcript of his interrogation."

"You got it, captain." Walsh barely moved as he reached for a file and tossed it in front of Holland. "I figured you'd want to see it, and that you'd want it old-school so I had a copy transcribed to this synthetic crap we still call paper."

Holland snatched it off the desk. "A pleasure as always, Lew."

"Don't be a stranger, Holland."

The captain turned and left.

"Oh Officer Hawke," Walsh called.

Bernie waited.

"Your wife's going to lose today. So sorry."

Holland found an empty nook and Bernie took a seat opposite him. As the captain read a page, he slid it over to Bernie. At the last one, he waited for the officer to catch up.

"Well?" Holland asked.

"I hate to say it," Bernie replied, "but Walsh has a point. Mobley is more afraid of whoever did this than he is of the police." Robin Hood? he wondered. Or Dirty Harry?

Holland shook his head. "So why'd they let him go? A stolen shipment of food in his warehouse. Three known felons found dead. That alone is enough to hold him."

"You think Walsh didn't put everything in the report?"

"I think he didn't ask the questions."

Bernie collected the papers, tapped them against the desk, and slid them back in the file. "I don't get it."

"Walsh wasn't worried about me at all. Someone's protecting him."

"Meaning?"

"The branches of this corrupt, gnarly tree reach higher than I thought." Holland stood. "We need to find Mobley before he ends up down in the morgue next to those hired guns."

Part II

Mechanical Chaos

13

"The universe is not mystical," Litz said into his vid com while struggling to control his anger. "And the world is not a haven for wizards and enchanters or spirits and mythical beasts. It is rock and water, bone and blood. It cares no more about you than it does about the faded writing on a tombstone. So you take your talk of this Robin Hood and you plant its bones in the dusty earth where it belongs. Do you hear me?"

"Senator," the man replied, his large bald head dominating the screen, "we don't make the news. We simply report it. And if people are calling him Robin Hood, then it's our job to investigate."

"It seems to me you're attempting to create a modern day legend."

"That's just not true."

"Then perhaps you're perpetuating lies for the sake of ratings. Or did you forget a number of soldiers, American soldiers, died during the raid."

"I've forgotten nothing of the sort," the man fired back. "And your accusations are not only false but offensive. Our story reported all the information we'd received at the time with the promise of more as details emerge."

"Let me remind you that GNN stands for Government News Network."

"While that is true, it doesn't represent individual censorship."

"Your job is to report what we tell you to report."

"My job is to report the news. The people have a right to hear—"

"The people don't give a damn. They don't believe half of the lies you put out there."

"You can control access to information, but you can't control what we report. Sir."

Litz smiled thinly. "Don't forget where your funding comes from, Mr. Chairman."

"With all due respect, you're not the only member of the senate."

Yes, Litz thought. You have your protectors. For now. "But I'm the one the others will follow," he replied. "Remember that." And he cut the connection.

"Robin Hood," he scoffed aloud. Houston had been ready to blow like so many other places and one quixotic act had diffused the southwest sector. Fools clinging to hope, leaning on the crutch of a dead religion, not realizing their prayers fell on the deaf ear of a mechanical universe.

Litz needed to bring their attention back to him.

A woman cleared her throat, and he looked up. "Congressman Bishop is here," she announced.

"Send him in." After she left, Litz stood and paced over to the window. Haze dulled the city. Robin Hood or not, the heat would eventually melt whatever temporary hope the masses felt, parched throats and empty bellies demanding a savior, not short term patchwork. He only hoped Isabelle had done her part.

Litz smiled broadly as J. Henry Bishop entered the office. A little stout, with a friendly countenance, J. Henry was both powerful and popular. His colleagues called him the happy warrior. Litz stretched out a hand. "Thank you so much, congressman, for meeting with me."

J. Henry met his grip. "My pleasure, senator."

"Please have a seat. Would you like a drink? Brandy? Sherry?"

"No, thanks, I still need to workout this afternoon."

"Ah, an exercise fanatic?" A weightlifter, Litz figured. His hair was thinning but Bishop carried himself like an athlete, an aging one, perhaps, but an athlete nevertheless. It helped the senator see what attracted Isabelle to the man.

The congressman patted his gut. "Just trying to keep the extra pounds off," he replied, and with a wink added, "I don't want anyone stealing Isabelle away from me."

Litz fielded the last comment cautiously. "Many men envy you, J. Henry. There's no doubt about that."

"Are you one of them, Leonard?"

Litz forced a laugh, deciding to let the bull pass through the cape as close to his body as possible without getting gored. "I admit I tried to sweep your young bride off her feet at dinner in New York, but it's obvious she's completely devoted to you."

J. Henry locked his fingers together and rested his hands on his belly. "Isabelle spoke highly of you. Perhaps it's because you're both relative newcomers to town."

Litz choked back a wince. Admittedly, he was a junior senator and didn't have the years in the system as J. Henry. However, he was hardly a newcomer. If anything he was the outsider on the inside, whereas J. Henry Bishop definitely represented the establishment. And right now, he needed someone from the establishment. "Yes, it must seem that way to you since we've never really sat down and talked."

"I wasn't always chairman of the Ways and Means Committee, either." J. Henry shifted in his chair, crossing a leg over his knee.

Litz raised a finger. "I've reached out to you more than once. And until now you've resisted. Why's that?"

"Maybe until now we haven't had anything to discuss."

Litz nodded. "Excellent. So you are interested."

"I don't necessarily disagree with what you want," J. Henry told him. "But you're asking me to spend a lot of political cash."

"A number of people in this town owe you."

"You'll be one of them."

"Silence the calls for a select committee investigation, push through the supplemental bill for the southwest desalination project, and you'll be well rewarded."

"It's flattering that you think I can kill an investigation," J. Henry stated.

"You have the speaker's ear. And while the senate majority leader doesn't think highly of me, you and he went to school together and, I believe, play racquet ball regularly."

"You've done your homework."

"I'd be remiss not to, given the respect you command by your colleagues, including me." Litz leaned forward. "You can do it."

The congressman uncrossed his legs and put his palms on his knees. "What reward is worth the risk?"

Litz couldn't hide his curiosity. "Didn't Isabelle tell you?"

"She preferred I hear it from your lips."

"I see. Congressman Bishop, I want you to be the first chairman of the soon-to-be formed Water Cartel."

14

"He was using you," J. Henry told his wife.

"Of course, dear. I'm not such a neophyte that I didn't recognize that, or the possibility of it, even before I met with him."

"I meant no offense."

"None taken, darling. Although at times I think you forget I'm not the innocent you first took me for." She smiled wryly. Their arms were locked as they strolled in the brightly lit underground tunnels filled with shops, restaurants, coffee houses, theaters and pubs, a haven for the elite out of public eye so not in its mind. Every so often they passed someone J. Henry knew, but rather than stop for a political chat he simply touched the brim of his fedora and they continued on. She'd bought the fedora for him, believing it would add an air of dignity; she'd been right. Yet when he'd first failed to stop and talk Isabelle had chided him. *No, I'm seeking your counsel,* he'd said. *For now everyone else can wait.* My counsel, she'd thought. Finally the partnership she'd been trying to forge was taking shape.

"Save the naiveté for my sister, poor thing," Isabelle continued. "Even as society crumbles around us, Maria Ashley contemplates a religious life. Can you imagine? Clinging to a ghostly past. Why it's nothing more than hiding from the present."

"Be careful of belittling creatures of the spirit, Isabelle. They tend to have the one thing most people these days lack, passion. And religious passion has started many a war in the sad time line of humanity."

"Perhaps, but I don't foresee Maria Ashley starting a war. She's no Buddhist ready to light herself on fire or a Christian martyr prepared to go on a hunger strike. It's the Robin Hoods of the world that begin wars."

"Ah yes, I heard of that peculiar incident. I agree. That kind of fire spreads quickly. And I'm not so sure we should extinguish it."

Isabelle stopped, causing J. Henry to do the same. They stood in front of a bakery, the tantalizing scent of freshly baked bread wafting in the air. "What are you saying?"

J. Henry waved a hand. "Look around you, Isabelle. We want for nothing, and because of that we're failing the people of this country. Leonard Litz has hit the nail on the head. Things need to change before we all go up in smoke like the dying forests of California."

"So you're going to help him?"

"I have to be honest. The man makes me nervous, Isabelle. He's considered extreme by even the most conservative. That his populist message has taken root has surprised and unnerved many in the party. His motives are hardly altruistic."

"Don't the ends justify the means?"

"The road to Hell is paved with those very means."

"I didn't think you believed in Hell, J. Henry."

"Oh, I do, darling. It's just not down here. It's up there." He pointed toward the catwalks above them. She recognized he meant the blistering outside heat, which she also understood was the key to her argument.

A clerk for Justice Daily emerged from the bakery and greeted J. Henry. The congressman touched the tip of his hat as Isabelle gently tugged his arm and they resumed walking. "Justice Daily likes his croissants," J. Henry commented.

"But as you said, something needs to be done," Isabelle prompted to recapture the subject at hand.

A deep sigh escaped him. "I'll be selling my soul to the Devil. There will be no going back."

"The power will be with the cartel, J. Henry."

"I already have power, my dear. If I didn't, Litz wouldn't have given me the time of day."

"Darling, as head of the cartel you can directly affect the change you want. Think of the hydroponic projects you've been championing. Once you control the water the Ag industry will have no choice but to follow your lead. Also, we both know the technology to shield us from the sun is ready for mass production. We could be living in sheltered cities, bubbles of comfort, not trapped underground like moles."

"It's still a power issue. The grid isn't there."

"Hydro, darling. Hydro." Again she stopped. "It all comes down to water."

"We can't force the agri-business to share their technology."

"Oh yes we can," she protested. "You can. Whoever controls the water will control the country. The days of the republic are numbered, J. Henry."

"Better not tell Leonard Litz that. It'll only empower him." They resumed walking. "Besides, I'm not sure I believe it."

"I was wrong. It's not the Robin Hoods who change the world, darling. It's the kings who lead their soldiers on a crusade."

He slid her a sideways look. "Why my dear Isabelle, I think you're more religious than you let on."

"Bite your tongue."

J. Henry laughed, and for once he sounded relaxed. That's when she knew the tide was turning.

"Perhaps you should be the politician," he said.

"When you seek my counsel, I wouldn't be doing you any favors not to give my honest opinion."

"You've learned the ways of this town quickly, my dear."

"I've had a great mentor," she replied, smiling up at him, while thinking that Leonard Litz said the same thing. And she was beginning to believe it. "Can I tempt you with a drink?" she asked, pointing to a cozy piano bar, a replica of a posh Twentieth Century establishment. It was like stepping back in time.

"You can tempt me with just about anything and get away with it, Isabelle."

"Oh, how you tease me," she said and playfully slapped his shoulder. However, in reality she was beginning to believe that as well.

15

Rex Fielder waited patiently while the senator vented. If the military had taught him anything it was that politicians needed to talk even when it meant stating the obvious or repeating themselves over and again. He'd already briefed the good senator on how they'd lost the shipment of food to this so-called Robin Hood who was nothing more than a weapon's runner with a soft heart. To Fielder's surprise, however, Litz didn't want him to go after the rogue.

"He's bush league, Colonel Fielder," Litz said finally. "We have a bigger pot to stir."

"He's supplying weapons to people out in the New Dust Bowl," the colonel pointed out. "We'll have to take him on sooner or later."

"Once we secure the inner border, the New Dust Bowl will be nothing more than a desert prison. A Wasteland for the refuge of humanity. This Robin Hood can rot out there along with the rest of them."

"Yes, sir."

"What's more important is where's Mobley?"

"I had Walsh release him. We're keeping an eye on him."

"Let's hope it's a better eye than you kept on the food."

Fielder felt his eye twitch. Litz didn't notice.

"I want trouble down there, colonel. And I don't want anyone saving the day this time."

"Yes, sir." Fielder understood the senator's basic philosophy. As long as society functions in more or less an orderly fashion, the masses remain conservative. In other words, resistant to change and without the need for a strongman to come in and clean up the mess.

"And once it breaks out, I want Mobley to have an accident. Unlike you, I don't trust he'll keep his mouth shut."

Fielder's wolfish jaw tensed.

Sensing this, Litz back-peddled. "I know you're a man of honor, but revolutions have casualties and accidents can be acts of nature."

"Sometimes a baby cast down river in a basket grows up to lead his people to freedom," Fielder warned.

"Mobley is no Moses."

"True."

"Keep me informed, General," Litz ordered.

"Colonel," he corrected politely.

"Not for long." And Litz signed off.

Fielder grinned. Instinctively he realized he'd be throwing in with a winner. Litz was on the move, developing from a man of words to a man of action. All he needed was a field of chaos to get more people to listen to him. But if he had a weakness, it was that Litz underestimated men like the modern day Robin Hood. Loose ends fray the fabric of victory.

He swiveled his desk chair and gazed out the window. Black Ops. That was the bottom line. The appeal of a movement such as this was not so much the promise of opportunity but the illusion one could get rid of an unwanted self. After all, it was only the wise or fortunate who didn't wish at one time or another to be someone else. Even Fielder lamented he'd not been given a healthier body. It still took a sharp eye to see it was betraying him, but soon it would become more apparent as it became more difficult for him to move around.

He sighed, put it out of his mind. There was nothing he could do about it. And the decay was slow moving, its full impact years away.

Fielder refocused on the present, on the bottom line. Black Ops. He'd done it before, which was why Litz had sought him out. Of course, he'd been well compensated, and it appeared he would be again.

General Fielder. Yes, he liked the sound of it.

It sounded like power.

16

Bear lugged the case of cutters from the hovercraft. He flipped it from his shoulder and gently set the crate on the parched ground. His contact eyed the bounty greedily, particularly when she pried open the top and verified its contents.

"Nice," she said.

"You expected anything less?"

"I was told you'd deliver, but seeing is believing."

Bear didn't know this one very well. Usually he dealt with a Scrap named Julius. But Julius had broken his leg in some kind of accident, at least according to the girl, and she had taken his place. Her name was Celeste, which he found ironic. Celeste, heavenly, at the gates of the Inferno.

"Tell me, love," he said, "what's a nice girl like you doing in Hell?"

"I'm not a nice girl."

"Indeed." Bear's expression remained deadpan, but inside he grinned. Scraps were a tough lot. They scratched out a living by scavenging and mining patches of centuries old refuse, mostly plastic, metals and, if they were lucky, glass. The reckless waste of previous generations had now grown valuable.

"Besides," she added, "the real Hell is in and around the cities. Everyone knows that sooner or later the government is going to shield them with their electro-mag tech. Create bubbles of paradise, if you believe the propaganda. But are they really protection against the sun? Or are they prisons, a place to practice mind control? After all, make a person comfortable, given him enough frivolous distractions, and you can herd him anywhere."

Spoken like a true Scrap, he thought. Unfortunately, her words held much truth.

"I just came from the city," Bear pointed out. "It's hardly paradise."

Celeste shrugged. "Things have to get worse before they get better." She was lean and spry with short, cropped hair, though her weather-worn face added ten years to her appearance. They were in the middle of nowhere, no one around except a pack of wild dogs in the distance. Cutter in hand, she aimed at the empty shell of an abandoned filling station. The building had long ago been picked clean. But there were still jagged edges of glass in the front window. Celeste fired the cutter, shattering the toothy remnants. "Nice," she repeated. "How did you get these?"

Bear frowned. "Really, love?"

The sun peered down on them like the eye of an angry nun, its brittle rays rapping the knuckles of their souls.

Celeste gave another short shrug and fired again at the spikes of glass, hitting more than she missed. "I heard they had another food riot in the city," she stated while admiring the cutter.

He didn't correct her. "Word travels quickly."

"The police are blaming an old priest."

"Balderdash!"

The girl replaced the cutter in her holster with the new model. "It makes sense, whether he had anything to do with it or not. Priests are usually free thinkers, in their own dogmatic way, and the government is out to bury as many free thinkers as they can."

"Are you the queen of conspiracy?" he quipped.

"No, the princess of reality."

"Marvelous," he chuckled, though he scarcely felt joyful. She was a peculiar Scrap. Chattier than most. And speak of free thinkers. "How do you know the authorities are blaming the priest?" After all, she had called it a food riot when it was nothing more than a mad dash for charity.

"I hear talk. We have some Brothers living out here, now. They're worried. But what do you care? You know him?"

"I've done business with him, yes."

"You've done business with everyone, Bear." Celeste went over to her speeder to retrieve a satchel. "Speaking of," she added, and tossed it to him. "Count it. It's all there."

Bear thumbed through the bills while keeping one eye on the girl. He didn't expect trouble, but he always planned for it. "Marvelous," he repeated, wondering how Scraps had come across such a thick wad of promissory notes. Maybe she really wasn't a nice girl.

Celeste strapped the cutters onto the back of her speeder. "It's been real."

"To say the least. Tell Julius I hope he mends soon."

"Nobody mends soon these days, Bear. Best we can do is push through the pain."

"Yes, if you're going through Hell, keep walking."

A rare smile touched the corners of her mouth. "I know, right?"

"An old compatriot said that during another period of unrest."

Celeste put on her helmet. Before lowering her goggles, Bear raised a finger. The gesture made the girl edgy and she lowered her hand toward her cutter.

"Relax, love," Bear said. "One more question, if you don't mind."

A slight nod, though the hand remained at her side.

"Where can I find these Brothers you've been speaking with?"

17

"Welcome to tonight's third and final presidential debate. I'm your moderator, Gene Simmons. We begin tonight with a question for President Webster. How do you plan to revitalize the economy while at the same time protect us from the devastating effects of climate change?"

"Thank you, Gene. Well, let me begin by saying that free trade remains a vital component for economic growth, and with our ties to the rest of the world we can all come up with a plan to deal with the devastating effects of climate change."

"That's a pack of lies!"

"Senator Litz, it's not your turn."

"Gene, it is my turn. The American people know it's my turn."

"Isolationism is not—" Webster started to say.

"Mr. President, you have obviously had one nostalgic martini too many. Change is here. Change is with us. The people are with me. I hear it all the time. They say, 'Senator Litz, you need to do something.' Well, I intend to. Unlike you, Mr. President, I will put America first. America now. America forever. Free trade is dead, just like your administration . . ."

18

The contents of the next two food convoys that were attacked weren't driven away in any old carbon-chewer. They were torched. The smell of burning meat filled the air. The hulls of the hovercrafts were scorched beyond recognition. The guards and drivers who didn't die in the strikes were discovered face down on the ground, shot in the back of the head. Outrage filled the streets.

Holland Copeland shook his head. He could understand hijacking a shipment to sell on the black market, or even to give to the poor. He couldn't understand simply destroying it when so many people weren't getting enough to eat. Hands locked behind his head, he leaned back in his chair.

"No, sir," Bernie Hawke was responding on the vid. "I haven't located Mobley. Men are stationed outside his home and office, as you ordered, but he hasn't shown up at either one. Looks like he's gone underground."

Or he's dead, Holland thought. "Very well." He glanced at the news screen mounted above the filing cabinet. Senator Litz was ranting, but the sound was muted. He made better sense this way. "I want you to interview the priest downtown." When Hawke started to protest, Holland put out a hand. He'd expected it, which was why he had the visual on. "I know he was brought in for questioning. But I want your take. As I've said before, you have good instincts."

"Yes, sir."

He hesitated before signing off. "By the way, how did Kelly's case go?"

Bernie glanced down and then forced himself to look back into the vid.

"She lost."

19

"This is crazy, my friends, crazy," Leonard Litz was saying to the country. "Americans can't get enough to eat, and now we have terrorists blowing up shipments of food. And what is the administration doing? Nothing. Not a damn thing.

"President Webster sits in the White House, dines on fine food and wine—you know it's true; I've seen the bills—and calls for another investigation. People are starving in the streets, real people like you and me starving, and he wants to investigate? Really? It's ridiculous. The harm that man is doing to this country is absolutely ridiculous.

"When I'm president, I won't investigate. I'll track those terrorists down and have them shot. Yes, I will. Leftwing terrorists. I'm sure of it. Probably communists. Radical free thinkers who believe anything goes. Free thinkers who are trampling on your rights. Your right to life, liberty, and the pursuit of happiness. And you know what happiness is? It's more than food on your table for your family. That should go without saying. Food in your belly. A basic necessity. And this administration is denying you that fundamental right. You should be worrying about other things—a brighter future for your children, adapting to climate change—not something so basic. So basic. And the president and his cronies gorge themselves at the taxpayers' expense. Can you believe that? Maybe it's not just the terrorists who should be shot. You know what I mean? Gorge themselves. It's Bacchanalia, pure and simple. Nero stuffs his face while Rome burns. . . ."

20

Bernie Hawke was surprised to see the crowd outside the church. For a moment he wondered if they'd come into another cargo of food. Quickly he learned that was what the people who gathered had hoped, too. But it was mere hope, not reality.

He found Father Bartholomew in his dingy office. The tile floor was scuffed and the walls grungy. The priest was on the vid, a model two or three generations behind even the crap the cops used, trying to scrounge up food donations.

"I know we were blessed before," he said, "but people are still hungry. One contribution of food, generous as it was, didn't solve the problem. The struggle is ongoing. Anything you can give will be greatly appreciated."

Bernie stepped into the narrow hallway to allow the priest at least semi-privacy while he solicited, no begged. Lean times had gotten leaner. He expected the father to have no better luck than Kelly had in court.

Surveillance vids, the documenting of daily life, would soon kick up a notch. He wondered if even semi-privacy was fast becoming a thing of the past.

"Come in, please," Bartholomew called. "Though for the life of me I can't imagine what more I can tell you."

Bernie sat on a metal folding chair in front of a battered desk. He took out his vid, opened a tab, and a holographic representation of the priest's report appeared."

"According to your statement," Bernie began, "the food was an anonymous gift." He looked up. "Tell me, how did it get here?"

"Well, a man dropped it off in a hovercraft. Said he was paid to deliver the contents to the church. My, oh my, but wasn't he surprised when he learned what he'd been hauling around. Naturally we gave him a portion."

"Naturally. The driver have a name?"

"As I told the other officer, or I think he might've been a sergeant. No matter. As I told the first policeman who questioned me, the driver never introduced himself."

"What'd he look like?"

"Young, Hispanic, average height and weight."

Bernie knew the priest was lying. But he was smooth, very smooth.

"He helped us unload and then went on his way," Bartholomew continued. "Shortly after that, word got around and the crowd started to form. Well, you know the madness that ensued next."

"And you didn't find the *donation* at all suspicious?"

"It was a godsend. I simply thought it a generous act of charity. I didn't know the food was tainted with the blood of dead men. Metaphorically, of course."

"Of course." Bernie closed the report. "You know, Father, I think you know more than you're letting on. I think you could tell me who anonymous is."

"Apparently he's Robin Hood."

"Don't toy with me, Father."

"Believe me, that is the farthest thing from my mind, young man. But if you're looking for more information, I can't help you. Unless, of course, you want me to make something up."

"No, I think there's been enough of that." Bernie stroked his jaw. "Hank Mobley," he said.

"I beg your pardon?"

"Do you know him?"

"Hank Mobley? No, never heard of him. Who is he?"

It was the first complete statement Bernie believed, said with a sincerity the others lacked. "The soul survivor in the slaughter at the warehouse where your supply of food came from," he replied. "Surely you listen to the news."

"I do as much as anyone. Or maybe half-listen since obviously the name didn't stick." Father Bartholomew inched forward. "Don't you find it interesting one man was left alive? You don't suppose he's Robin Hood, do you?"

And now we were back to the shell game. "Only if he knocked himself unconscious and bound himself afterward."

"I see." He rested his arms on the desk, hands twined together. "I guess Mr. Mobley wasn't able to offer any insight into the identity of Robin Hood, or else you wouldn't be here."

Bernie took a chance. "Mr. Mobley claims that you know Robin Hood personally. That's why the food ended up here as opposed to the countless other places it could've gone."

For a moment the priest grew flustered. "Why would he claim such a thing?"

"Because it's true," Bernie pushed.

"Preposterous."

"Who's Robin Hood?"

"I haven't the faintest idea."

"And where's Hank Mobley?"

"Again, I don't know the man."

"Very well." Bernie stood. He tossed a card down on the desktop. "If you hear from either one, or you want to clear your conscience, call me."

"I surely will, officer." He eyed the card. "Oh, and Officer Hawke?"

"Yes, Father?"

"Any donation would be very welcomed."

Bernie looked at him like he'd lost his mind. Then he sighed and left a fiver in spite of himself.

21

Congressman J. Henry Bishop caught up with the presidential candidate on the campaign trail. Litz was half an hour away from addressing a crowd in Des Moines. Farmers with dry cows and parched fields. J. Henry knew Litz's approach. Promise what the voters want to hear, even though the days of the family farm were all but over as Big Ag was sucking the aquifers dry, and the cost of their genetically modified seeds was out of reach for most individuals. But if you give people hope of returning to past glories, they'll follow you anywhere. It hardly matters if it's realistic.

J. Henry continued to have reservations about Leonard Litz. But a crises was looming. Water was the future. And desalination provided an answer. The logjam in congress needed to be broken before it was too late.

He met Litz in a hotel room. The senator had ushered everyone out except for his chief strategist, Mitch Skyler. Skyler was young and ambitious and many people deluded themselves by thinking he tempered Litz's extremism. J. Henry knew better. Skyler was a toady who expected to be well rewarded for his loyalty.

"Ah, Congressman Bishop," Litz said, "thank you for traveling all the way out here. Do you know Mitch Skyler?"

"I do." He met the young man's hand but said nothing more.

"Please sit," Litz added.

J. Henry settled on a couch with Litz in a matching chair facing him. Skyler muted a vid, another GNN report of civil unrest, and remained standing.

"So what's so important you felt the need to meet face-to-face?" Litz

60

asked.

"Less likely to be overheard or have information leaked, senator."

"OK. What do you have for me?"

J. Henry inched forward. "Good news and bad news. First the good news. There won't be a select committee investigating misappropriation of funds for the southwest desalination plant. Both the speaker and majority leader agree it would be a waste of taxpayer money."

Litz grinned. "Very good. So what's the bad news?"

"President Webster is threatening to veto any supplemental spending bill aimed at restarting the project. And as you know, he and I don't exactly see eye-to-eye, so it appears my influence stops here. We don't have the support to override a veto." J. Henry waited, expecting to experience the famous Litz anger. Instead the senator remained surprisingly calm.

"Push the bill through, congressman. Let me worry about the president."

J. Henry stood. "Very well."

A knock interrupted them. Litz turned to Skyler, who opened the door. "The senator will be out in a minute," Skyler said.

"We have a situation," an aid stated.

"We're wrapping it up."

"This can't wait."

"Let her in," Litz ordered. "What is it Mallory?" he asked after the young woman stepped past Skyler.

"There's been an explosion in Detroit," she announced. "It happened at the convention center just as Governor Powell was starting to speak."

Litz grew serious. "Is the governor all right?"

"We don't know. Initial reports are that he's been taken to a local hospital."

J. Henry had met the governor before but didn't know him very well. He'd been a below-the-radar pick as Litz's running mate. Many pundits thought it was because he might be able to deliver Michigan. J. Henry figured it was because Powell was easily controlled.

"Find out what's going on," Litz ordered Skyler. He nodded and left the room.

"The Secret Service want to cancel the rally," Mallory said.

"I'll not be a hostage to terrorism."

"Then delay it," J. Henry pointed out. "Gather all the information you can."

Litz looked from Mallory to the congressman and back. "Yes, delay it until we know what's going on."

"Yes, sir." The aid left.

"Senator," J. Henry said, "if there's anything I can do."

"Thank you. Just get the supplemental spending bill through the house. I'll be in touch."

As the flurry of activity picked up, J. Henry quietly left. He was not needed here. Instinctively he felt Governor Powell was dead, though he didn't know how this would affect the election.

However, he would soon find out, not realizing then the role he was about to play.

22

Holland Copeland rubbed his eyes. Just looking at Litz made him weary, and now this, the senator's running mate assassinated. "What do you make of it?" he asked.

Bernie poked at his food and shook his head.

Kelly Hawke took a bite of chicken and chewed slowly.

Neither said anything. Holland realized he should've turned off the news while they ate. He'd invited them over to his house a week ago. Dumb luck this turned out to be the night. GNN replayed portions of Litz's speech in Des Moines, which had begun solemnly and ended with a fiery attack on the current administration and a call to action against the rising tide of homegrown terrorists. The GNN anchors added commentary and interviewed various pundits, though little information on who was behind the bombing had come out. Finally Holland picked up the controller and turned the broadcast off.

"Leonard Litz just won the presidency," Kelly stated.

Bernie stopped prodding his food. "How do you figure?"

"Part sympathy vote, but more importantly, it shows Webster as weak. Americans don't like weak."

"You can't blame Webster for that," Bernie protested.

"It doesn't help we don't know who did it," Holland added. "But I'm not so sure it wins him the office. Litz is kind of out there. I think it depends on who he picks to replace Powell."

Kelly forked another piece of chicken. "I don't think the choice of a running mate matters," she countered, "unless something like this happens." She ate and pointed at Bernie's food with her fork. "Eat," she encouraged. "This is a treat. Thank you, Holland."

"My pleasure." He'd slaughtered and dressed one of his chickens and roasted potatoes with rosemary and carrots as a side dish. Holland would be the first to admit he was far from an accomplished cook. Deborah had the touch when it came to anything culinary. What he'd learned had been pure dumb luck, a type of osmosis from the sheer number of years they'd been together. He wished they were still together.

"Still haven't located Mobley," Bernie said to change the subject.

"Funny you should mention that," Holland replied. "I had an idea. You can bet Lew Walsh knows where Mobley's hiding out, and he's keeping a close eye on him. So pick up one of his men and tail him. It might take a few tries but sooner or later we'll know where he is, too."

"He's not going to talk to you," Kelly told them.

"You're probably right," replied Holland. "But we can let him know that we're here, and that we can find him."

"Of course, if he's the connection to something bigger your finding him might put him in danger," Kelly pointed out.

"That's a chance we're just going to have to take."

Bernie buttered a roll. "I still think it was just a deal gone bad. If Lew Walsh was anything more than a sleazy opportunist don't you think Mobley would be part of the new desalination plant?"

"And you still might be right," Holland agreed. "But we won't know until we get a crack at him. And I want a crack at him. Deals gone bad don't leave survivors, unless they're valuable."

"That's what Kelly said."

"So why is Mobley valuable?" Holland asked.

"Money," responded Kelly. "Doesn't it always come down to money?"

"And power," Bernie added.

As if on cue, the power cut out and the ranch house went dark for a few seconds before the generator clicked into gear and the security lights flashed on.

Holland grinned and tipped his beer bottle in a toast. "The desire for it," he told them. "That's for sure."

23

"Isabelle, how nice to hear from you."

"Thank you for taking my call, Senator. I realize how valuable your time is."

"You're quite welcome. What can I do for you?"

She took a deep breath. "My husband is putting his career on the line for you."

"Oh?"

She heard the famous Litz edge, razor sharp, and pushed forward. "Tell me what I'm hearing isn't true."

"What are you hearing, my dear?"

"You're thinking of offering the VP position to Fitzsimmons."

"Congressman Fitzsimmons is a solid choice. Now please, allow the professionals to do their job. Besides, I've already said I'd make J. Henry the first chairman of the Water Cartel."

"It'll take years for the Water Cartel to get off the ground." She didn't know if this was true or not, and she realized it went against what she'd earlier told her husband, but she sensed an opportunity and instinctively pursued it. "In the meantime, he'll be in political limbo," she added.

"It is a very powerful office."

"So is the vice presidency."

She heard him pause. The ultimate establishment feather in his cap. He was considering it.

"Would he accept?" Litz asked.

"Why would he not?"

"Did J. Henry put you up to this?"

"He'd be horrified to know I called. And then grateful."

"Oh, Isabelle, what am I to do with you?"

She heard the smile in his voice.

"Dance with me at the inaugural ball, of course."

24

With the cutters disposed of, Bear had traded out the small hovercraft for his speeder and now he approached the rocky outcropping cautiously. The peculiar Scrap, Celeste, had pointed him in this direction. Yet he wasn't sure if it was accurate information or simply a method to shake loose from him.

At first glance, the land appeared desolate, hardly a place to set up camp. A patch of green-brown scrub oak and mesquite clung to the earth near a crown of pink granite. They looked like the talons of a great bird digging into the rosy scalp of an old monk. How very Greek, Bear thought. An apocalyptic Prometheus.

Close up, though, he noticed an entrance behind the sparse vegetation, evidently marking a cave beneath the ledge of rock. How deep or shallow it went, he couldn't tell, but it certainly offered a respite from the brittle sun. Bear dismounted his speeder and drew his cutter.

"Hello in the cave," he called. Though technically Bear hadn't hit the Wasteland, or the New Dust Bowl as the media had initially called it back in the city, the Wasteland was expanding and even on its outskirts, dens such as this were precious. It wouldn't be surprising to find that someone less reputable had suggested a pair of brothers look for lodging elsewhere. "Hello," he repeated.

"Come in peace," a voice called back.

"I'll do my best. I'm called Bear."

"I know the name, not the man."

"Show yourself and you'll know both."

America Unbalanced

Two men emerged. One was short and lean with a tuft of curly dark hair. The other was heavyset and almost as tall as Bear. He had a wide, plain face and thinning brown hair. Something about the larger of the two didn't seem quite right. Both were dressed in khaki shirts and pants, rather than any type of robes, and they appeared unarmed.

"I'm Brother Xavier," the shorter man said. "This is Brother Francis. You don't need that weapon."

I'll be the judge of that, he thought. "You don't look like brothers."

"We've found that people are more willing to let us approach them if we don't seem to be asking for a handout."

"Are you?" Bear asked and holstered the cutter.

"Not without providing a service first."

"Which is?"

"Salvation of the soul, my good man."

"Salvation of the soul in a soulless land. You're on a fool's mission, Brother."

"No mission in the name of the All Mighty is foolish."

Bear found it curious that Xavier did all the talking, though it confirmed that Father Bartholomew would find comfort with them. "Well, Padre, I'll make a bargain with you."

"Ah, is the Devil tempting me in the desert? After all, your reputation precedes you."

"Only offering to share a meal in return for a few hours out of this sun, and on the condition you leave my soul to me."

"Shade I can give you. But I can't swear that a concern or two about your eternal spirit won't slip off my tongue."

Bear chuckled. "Marvelous."

Brother Francis tugged on his thick lower lip. "You've come to ask us for something," he stated, catching Bear by surprise. "It has to do with a priest in the city."

Xavier, observing Bear's reaction, said, "If you take the time to get to know us, you'll realize that Francis is different. What most people read as mental slowness is actually far from it."

"Different, you say. Is he mad?"

"Some would say so. On the other hand, I'd venture you and he have more in common that you might think. But come, you didn't find us by accident."

"No, I didn't." Bear thought of the feisty young Scrap. "Frankly, Brother,

68

I believe your guardian angel sent me. Bit of a fallen angel, but guardian nonetheless."

"Really? And what is this angel's name?"

"It's not important."

"Well, whoever it was must have seen we have a lot to learn. No doubt you could teach us a thing or two about the Barrens and Wasteland." Xavier's eyes narrowed. "Of course, Brother Francis could be your teacher as well."

25

J. Henry Bishop was stunned. He punched off the vid and paced in the den of his Georgetown home. How had he not seen this coming? His political instincts normally kept him a step ahead of most people. Now he was at a crossroads, only he felt like an immigrant dropped in the middle of an unknown land. The choice he made now had the potential to shape the rest of his life, and it had to be made quickly.

"What is it, darling?"

Isabelle's voice drew him from his thoughts. "I just spoke with Leonard Litz. He wants me to be his new running mate. Did you know about this?"

"Of course not," she replied quickly. Her hand went to her throat as she took a couple of steps into the room. "What did you tell him?"

"I had to think about it. Naturally, though, he wants to act fast." He stepped from behind his massive oak desk to the window that looked out over the backyard. Pushing back the plush red curtain, he gazed out at the greenhouse that supplied them a generous amount of fresh produce. Robert, his chief gardener, saw him and waved. He didn't make much of a salary, but the food bonus and cabin on the grounds where he and his family stayed more than made up for the low wages. However, if the press got hold of this, they'd have a heyday. He acknowledged Robert's wave and let go of the curtain.

"What about being the first chairman of the Water Cartel?" Isabelle asked.

"He didn't close the door on it," J. Henry replied. "But he's scrambling, after Powell's death."

Isabelle went up to J. Henry's desk and put a hand on it as if to steady herself. "He needs someone on the ticket who's strong."

"He needs someone who'll legitimize his candidacy and calm the skeptics."

"But he's not an outsider. He's a senator."

"Who's been on the fringe and made a lot of enemies. Isabelle, I never wanted to leave the House of Representatives."

"Sometimes Fate demands that you step it up, darling."

"I'm not so sure I believe in Fate, dear."

"History, then. You're a student of it. Think of how many times History has asked ordinary people to do extraordinary things. And you, J. Henry, are not ordinary." She went to him and touched first his shoulder and then his face.

"You think I should accept?"

"I think it's your duty."

"I won't be able to accomplish as much as I could as head of the cartel."

"That time may still come, but think of it this way. You won't be able to accomplish anything if Litz loses. As powerful as you are in the house, it'll be more of the same, fighting with Webster. And he won't forgot how you killed the call for a select committee to investigate misappropriation of funds for the southwest desalination plant."

J. Henry nodded. "Fair point." Strange, but in nixing the call, he'd learned it had been less a misappropriation of funds and more of a conflict of interest. The contracts went to Litz-connected companies. Since he'd protected Litz on that one, the senator must believe he could do it in other areas, too.

Isabelle kissed his cheek and patted his heart. "Take the night to consider it. But for what it's worth, I think this is a call you have to make."

"I value your opinion. You have good instincts."

"So do you, darling."

He drew a deep breath. He wished that was so because then he wouldn't feel so conflicted.

26

It took Bernie Hawke a couple of days but finally he shadowed the right cop. He knew he had a live one when a robbery call not far from their location went unheeded. The officer traveled with a purpose, pulling to a stop outside a shabby apartment complex. Surrounding it was commercial storefront, though you could count the number of businesses that remained open on one hand. Much of the brick and mortar had layers of graffiti, each new tag re-tagged by a rival gang. Clusters of people wandered, looking for anything they could take, hoping for something to eat, or they leaned against these buildings of abandoned dreams stoned out of their minds. Food might be hard to come by, but drugs never were.

The apartment complex was gated, though Bernie suspected the gates were more for psychological purposes than practical. Walsh's cop keyed in a number and the gate swung open. Bernie watched the unmarked hovercraft round a corner and he waited, resisting the urge to rush in and draw attention to himself. Eventually he trailed an incoming speeder, who paid him no mind.

The unmarked craft was parked outside a three-story row of units. Bernie stopped about a football field away and looked through his spyglasses. The cop was a woman dressed in civilian clothes. Bernie found that odd. Mobley had to know he was under surveillance. Why bother to hide it?

Bernie also noticed that the officer was young, Hispanic, and attractive. Curiously, she put on lipstick and took off her dark jacket, showing a sleeveless lilac colored top. When she stepped out of the hovercraft, she smoothed a short, black skirt, opened a small purse and peeked inside, then snapped it close. She scanned the parking lot. It remained inactive, and she paid no attention to Bernie. If he didn't know any better, Bernie would've said a little tryst was going on. But he did know better. He set the spyglasses down and got out of the craft.

Her back was to him. She went up a flight of stairs. Bernie jogged close to the building, beneath the long walkway above. When he came to the stairs, he stopped. He hadn't heard any knocking or a door open. Bernie inched his way to the landing on the second floor. Risking a glance left then right, he saw that the long, open corridor was empty. He went up to the third level and found her. She stood waiting about four or five apartments to his left.

Before Bernie could decide what to do next, a door swung open. When a man stepped out, the woman went into her act. She stared distraughtly at a door.

"Are you all right?" he asked. Mobley had the look of a cheap character actor in a bad gangster flick, Bernie decided. Not fat but not trim, either, receding hairline, and wearing a suit that didn't fit quite right.

"Oh, I just moved in and can't remember my code."

"Just moved in? A pretty girl like you? What's wrong, are you on the lam?" he asked laughing.

"Goodness, no," she replied, forcing a laugh of her own. "Unless you count trying to get on my feet after a recent divorce."

"That's tough. Sorry."

"Don't be. I'm glad he's out of my life, and I'm ready to move on." Her voice dropped slightly at the last sentence. "Now if I could only get inside my apartment."

"Don't you have your transmitter?"

"It's inside, of course."

"Well, you can call the super. I'm sure he can give you the code."

"And my vid's inside, too."

"This is not your day, ah . . ." he let his voice trail off.

"Esmeralda. But everyone calls me Esme."

"Well, Esme, I'm Hank. Would you like to call the super from my apartment?"

"That would be very nice, Hank. Thank you."

Hank, you dumb, horny bastard, Bernie thought. As Mobley keyed in his code, Bernie took the last two steps and came up behind them, cutter drawn.

Mobley opened his door, too focused on Esme's strapless top to notice she'd unsnapped her purse and was reaching inside it, or to realize that Bernie had quietly approached them.

"Drop it," he ordered, pressing his cutter against the back of the young woman's head.

"Hey, what the hell?" Mobley barked. "You're messing with the wrong person, cowboy."

Esme froze.

"I'm a cop," Bernie told her. "And I don't care how good you are, but nobody misses this close."

"You don't know what you're doing, cop," Esme said. Her flirty voice had turned cold as a gravestone.

"Really? I believe I'm keeping you from killing this man."

"From what?" Mobley asked.

"Oh, Hank, wake up. She is so out of your league."

"Turn around and leave," Esme told Bernie.

"So who ordered it?" Bernie asked. "I know it isn't Walsh's idea. He's just someone's lackey. The question is, whose lackey?"

The attractive woman didn't respond. She stood without moving, as calm as if he had a brush against her hair rather than a weapon.

"I didn't really expect an answer," Bernie continued. "I'm thinking out loud more than anything."

"You're not thinking at all, cop."

"Captain Copeland will be very interested in meeting you," he added. "And you, too, Mr. Mobley."

Mobley had paled, the sudden shift in the situation finally hitting home. "Why would they do this to me?" he asked.

"Who are they?"

Mobley's mouth was open but no words came out.

"Nevertheless a good question. Maybe we can figure that out together." Bernie unclipped a pair of cuffs from his belt.

"Don't listen to him," Esme told Mobley. "I was sent to protect you."

Mobley shook his head. "No. You're lying. If you'd been sent to protect me you wouldn't have made up that whole story about being locked out."

"Hands behind your back," Bernie told her, once more pushing the cutter against her head. "Come on, Esme, if that's really your name. I'd hate to splatter your pretty brains all over Mr. Mobley."

Esme obeyed, lowering her hands toward him. He intended to secure the assassin. She was the more dangerous of the two. He could handle Mobley once unknotted from Esme. With one hand, Bernie slapped a cuff on her left wrist. But as he lowered the cutter and glanced down to secure the right cuff, all hell broke loose.

Mobley used the moment of Bernie's distraction to grab a desk lamp and swing it at the entangled couple. Esme took the brunt of it, the base glancing off the side of her head. But it also clipped Bernie in the nose. Esme dropped to the floor, knocking the cutter from Bernie's hand. He grabbed his throbbing nose, feeling the blood between his fingers, before he got his bearings back and picked up the cutter. He turned to fire but Mobley was out of the apartment.

Esme lay motionless on the floor. Bernie went after Mobley.

Blood ran down his face and if he drew a breath through his nose he could taste it on the back of his throat. Mobley had already reached ground level.

"Stop," Bernie ordered.

Of course he didn't. Mobley sprinted across the lot, the sound of his shoes echoing against the ancient pavement.

"Stop," Bernie ordered again. The suspect kept running. From the second story landing, Bernie squeezed off a couple blasts. They missed, only adding more potholes to the already disheveled lot. Mobley rounded a corner, out of site.

Bernie followed, but Mobley had disappeared. He searched blindly for a short time before deciding he needed help. A hot trail quickly grew cold.

Blood stained his fingers. After putting in the call, he continued to weave in and out of the apartment buildings. No Mobley. Finally he gave up and waited for the cavalry.

When he returned to Mobley's flat, he discovered Esme was gone, too. He realized in the mêlée he hadn't secured the second cuff.

Great, he thought. Lost the witness. Let an assassin go free. And the only thing he had to show for it was a busted nose. Holland Copeland would have a thing or two to say about this.

And he did.

27

"In these dangerous times," Leonard Litz told the audience in Dallas, Texas, "we need leaders who will be honest with the American people, who will tell it like it is and not what the polls say people want to hear."

"Yeah!" someone yelled from the audience. It was followed by a burst of applause.

"Yeah is right. Thank you. Now first I want to express my condolences to Governor Powell's family. He was a good man, a good man, and a close friend. He would've made a hell of a vice president. But God didn't have that in mind for him. You know, I think of God as kind and loving, but unfortunately we don't live in a kind and loving world. Governor Powell's murderers will be caught and punished. I guarantee it. I don't turn the other cheek.

"I'll miss Governor Powell, I surely will. However, he would've been the first to say we have to soldier on. This election is bigger than any one man, any one person. So I've asked a good friend of mine, someone you're all familiar with, to step in and fill Governor Powell's shoes. And I'll be honest with you. Representative J. Henry Bishop was hesitant, but you know me. I can be persistent. When I want something, or someone, I don't stop until I get it. And Representative Bishop recognized that there are times in history when duty calls, when your country calls, and you have to answer. You have to. America first, my friends. Tighten the borders. Food in. Pandemic out.

"So it is my pleasure to introduce you to the next vice president of the United States, my dear friend and trusted advisor, Representative J. Henry Bishop.

"Come on up here, Representative Bishop. Listen to those applause. Aren't they beautiful? We love you. Thank you. Thank you. Come on up, Representative Bishop, and maybe you can answer a question we've all been wondering about. What does the J stand for, anyway? I think it stands for justice. Justice for Governor Powell. Justice for America. What do you think, folks?

"Thank you. Thank you. You're too kind."

28

"What happened?" Colonel Rex Fielder asked.

Lew Walsh wiped the sweat from his forehead. "A special forces officer showed up."

"You mean your person was followed."

"I don't know how it happened."

"Of course you don't." Fielder eyed the glass of scotch in front of him. He wasn't much of a drinker. After all, only a fool opens the door of his mind to a 90 proof vampire. Yet they were in a jazz dive. He needed to keep up appearances.

"We'll find Mobley," Walsh stated, tossing back his drink without so much as a grimace. He signaled for another.

The lighting was dim. The air smelled of sweat and cheap liquor. A trio started a new set. Fielder leaned across the table so he could be heard. "You'd better. The time has come to tie up loose ends. And Hank Mobley is an end that could unravel the tapestry of a whole campaign."

"Relax, I've got this."

The waitress approached and replaced the lieutenant's empty glass with a full one.

"Come on," Walsh added, "didn't we crank up the rioting like you wanted?"

"What about the church?"

"That was just dumb luck."

Fielder turned the glass without lifting it. "I don't think so." Contrary to what Litz said, the colonel wanted to send Robin Hood a signal.

"What do you want? I can't arrest the priest. He ain't done nothing."

"When has that ever stopped you?" Fielder raised the glass, sniffed the scotch, and decided turpentine would go down easier. He set it back down without drinking.

"The priest has got friends." Walsh tossed down his second drink.

"So have I."

"I know, I know." He caught the waitress's eye and pointed to his empty glass. "I guess we could let it out that they got another shipment of food and see what happens."

"See, I knew you could use your brain for something other than a repository for bad booze. You do that. And you find Mobley." He pushed the scotch across the table to Walsh.

"I told you I got this." The lieutenant looked at the offering then shrugged his shoulders and drank. "Not the best in the world, but it does the trick."

Fielder grinned. Only a fool opens the door of his mind to a 90 proof vampire. When the time came, he would take care of this loose end personally.

29

Bear had a bad feeling. And hanging around the two greenhorn brothers only exacerbated the feeling.

He couldn't explain why he didn't leave them to their own devices. At best, there might be a day in the future when they'd be able to offer him a place to stay during his travels. Nothing more. Frankly, Bear doubted even that. Their chances of survival were slim.

Xavier was arrogant, blindly following a deity that long ago had given up on this world. Or rather that the world had given up on. Either way, the thin margins of his dogma rigidly defined him.

Francis was different. He too trusted in the unseen, but he appeared less restricted by any doctrine, which Bear understood. Since he could remember, Bear had possessed a certain sight. However, he'd also learned not to ignore what was right in front of his face. The everyday grounded Bear, and it seemed to do the same for Francis, though he'd wager that the odd brother leaned more on the visions that came to him whereas Bear didn't completely trust either side. Visions could be misread, and quite often not everything was as it appeared to be in this so-called reality.

"You cannot stay here," Bear told them. "Outcroppings such as this are meant for layovers. Sooner or later you'll run out of provisions. And you can't rely on the charity of the desperate, which is pretty much all you'll find out here."

Francis tugged on his lower lip and said nothing. Xavier drank tea. It was early morning. A red sun bled across the horizon. Against his better judgment, Bear was grilling some of the meat he'd acquired from Father

Bartholomew. His initial plan had been to make jerky so he could ration it. The two men, though, while uncomplaining, were obviously half-starved, prompting Bear to give in to his soft side.

"What do you suggest?" Xavier asked.

"That you move closer to town. Granted, the cities are no longer safe, and the suburbs are in ruins. But I've noticed people are settling on the outskirts, rimming the municipalities, as it were. I suspect this will create a sort of buffer zone between proper society and the Wasteland. If you insist on proselytizing out here, it may provide a safe base from which to work."

"Your advice is grounded on much supposition," Xavier pointed out.

"Very true. But the chaos we're going through will lead to conformity. I see cities somehow becoming gated communities for the rich, and for those who line up behind them."

"Society needs order, does it not?"

Bear turned the steaks over, the sizzling verbal taunts to their hunger. "But this new order we're coming to will mean the death of democracy."

"You overreact, my friend." Xavier sipped his tea. "That is one thing I've discovered here. Conspiracy theories abound."

"Be that as it may, Brother, a corporate oligarchy is coming. It's always been there, a bit hidden in back-room politics, but it will soon be front and center, led by our very own Leonard Litz."

"I have no patience for politics, my friend. There's a higher power to follow."

"Perhaps you're right. But remember, a single man can cause much damage, and sometimes for as little a reward as a few pieces of silver."

Xavier lifted his tea then stopped halfway to his mouth. Bear thought he'd scored a point until a low growl caught his attention. The sizzling had stirred more appetites than their own. A pack of wild dogs had ventured close. Without hesitating, Bear stood, drew his cutter, and killed two of them. Starvation, however, trumped fear and the lead dog charged. Bear took careful aim and fired, felling the leader inches from the fire. The pack scattered.

"So you see, this is a country of many dangers. Damn wild dogs are becoming more of a problem, their fear of people nonexistent." He holstered his cutter, grabbed the dead dog by the nape of its neck and hoisted it aside. If only all threats were as easily disposed of. Of course, Bear pondered, Leonard Litz was probably thinking the same thing.

Bear divvied up the meat. The brothers had little to offer except a few stale corn tortillas. Before eating, Francis gave thanks. Bear waited respectfully.

America Unbalanced

For a few minutes they ate in silence. The sun slowly hoisted its thick body over the horizon, its hot anger spreading like lies through an ignorant electorate. A tortilla split in half when Bear tried to wrap it around a piece of meat. He sopped it in some juices and consumed it nonetheless.

"You must bring him to us," Francis stated.

Bear glanced up from his plate. He'd been thinking that Litz was going to scorch us all. As much as he hated politics, and didn't have a lick of faith in any leader, his mind annoyingly returned time and again to the thought of Litz running the country. So Francis's out of the blue statement caught him off-guard.

"Come again, mate."

"It has already begun," Francis replied. "If he remains in the city, he will not survive. His church is no longer a sanctuary. But you already know this, which is why you carry your anger."

No one had looked into him with such acuteness since his mother, God rest her soul. She'd followed a very old path. Francis, Bear felt sure, did not travel the same path, though he'd always suspected that many trails arrived at the same end.

For once Xavier had nothing to add. In fact, Bear felt the little brother studying him, awaiting his reaction.

"These are angry times, Brother Francis," he responded, ducking the gist of what he'd said.

Francis nodded, his wide face impassive, his large body rocking as well. "Times made angrier when a man is unwilling to take action for what he believes in. Do you think you honor your mother's memory by giving away food? Large or small?" He tapped his plate with his fork.

"Why you ungrateful sot."

Francis shook his head. "Ungrateful? No. I give thanks for this meal, even if it derives from an act of self-deception."

"Self-deception?" Bear repeated, his deep voice growing loud.

"You feed your conscience, allowing you the space to pursue your desires."

Bear controlled his anger only because they were brothers and his respect for the spiritual ran deep. Had Francis been a Scrap, he'd have beaten him senseless.

Xavier reached over and touched the large brother on the sleeve. "I think that's enough."

Francis closed his thick-lidded eyes and gently chewed the last bite of his food.

Bear finished his plate and stood. "You'd do well to follow my advice and move into the Rim. There's nothing but pain and suffering out here." He wiped his plate and started packing his belongings.

"No, Francis and I have already decided to go north. After all, we're in the business of pain and suffering."

"You'll not find paradise," he told Xavier.

"We don't expect to. But we believe somewhere there's a space where we can begin to carve out a new community."

"Marvelous," Bear retorted dryly. "Then may God help you."

"Oh, He will," Xavier answered. "I can only pray the same for you. As you've experienced, Francis has a way of getting under people's skin. I said he could be your teacher. I didn't say it would be pleasant, or even a success. That's for you to decide. Regardless, we know which way we're travelling. Do you?"

Part III

Divine Brutality

30

The church burned.

Christ, with his crown of thorns, nailed to his tree, went up in flames.

A rumor had spread that they were hoarding food. Father Bartholomew had invited the press into the pantry to prove how sparse an inventory they kept, but it didn't matter. People ignored the evidence and listened to the propaganda. The pantry was a front. They really had vaults filled with food beneath the rectory. Or maybe beneath the sanctuary. The pope was wealthy. All Catholic churches had vaults of food. And as the rumor went, they intended to use it in order to control the government and, in turn, the American people.

Bernie Hawke arrived as local police in riot gear were breaking up the crowd, firing teargas and Taser blasts while they protected the firefighters who attempted to save the church. Teargas, he thought. And Taser jolts. Technology had moved on but some departments hadn't. Bernie had seen Active Denial System Antennas, or ADSA, in action. It was like a shaft of energy from a human microwave because it warmed the liquid in a body, and no amount of resisting worked. Crowds broke, people backed away. Effective shields to combat the waves had yet to be designed. So it was an efficient and relatively harmless system, but some still seemed to favor good old-fashion brutality.

However, Bernie hadn't returned to the church because of the riot or even to check on the priest. Rather, he'd received a tip that Mobley had come in this direction.

Captain Copeland had not been happy that Mobley had slipped through the cracks, although he understood if Bernie had waited for backup their witness would probably be dead. On the other hand, Bernie had felt the sting of losing the assassin through the captain's laconic directions. With Esme in custody, it was quite likely they'd have gotten to the bottom of who was behind the hit.

Emergency lights slashed against the night's dark chaos. Radio chatter crackled. Muffled shouts and screams clashed with the buzz of Tasers and the pop of good old-fashion gunfire. Water, precious water, pounded the fire and puddled on the cracked ground. Bernie could smell the moisture in the humid air. He found the command craft and identified himself. A gruff old lieutenant stared at him. "Special Forces? You think you're taking over?"

"I wouldn't want your job."

"That makes two of us." He pointed at the bandage on Bernie's nose. "What happened to you?"

"An argument with my wife," he quipped.

"She must have a hell-of-a right hook. What do you want?"

"I'm looking for Father Bartholomew, the priest of this parish."

"And I'm looking for some peace and quiet. Guess neither one of us is going to get what we want tonight."

It was Bernie's turn to stare.

"Look, kid," the lieutenant eventually said, "by the time we got here the church was an inferno and people were busting windows and carrying off anything that wasn't nailed down."

"So you don't know if anyone was inside?"

"If there was, they'd have been smart to run out the back door and keep running. Now if you'll excuse me, Special Forces Officer Hawke, I have a situation to handle. It'll be morning before we get things under control and begin bagging bodies. I hope you find your priest before then, but if you don't, you might want to check back."

Bernie left the lieutenant responding to a call. Near one of the fire crafts he found a couple of sooty fighters with their hoods off, sweat rolling down their faces, drinking water. Again he identified himself and asked, "Was anyone in there?" For a long moment they stared through him as if they'd heard something but weren't quite sure where the sound had come from. "I'm looking for a priest," he added.

The smaller of the two, a woman, Bernie realized, focused her attention on him and shook her head. "Can't tell you. We had to wait for the cops to clear the mob before we could attack the fire. By then the flames climbed high into the night, to light the sacrificial rite, and I saw Satan laughing with delight."

The world was making everyone mad, he thought, or exhausted to the point of delusion. He gave her the benefit of a doubt. "A poet firefighter?"

Her partner gave a tired laugh. "She's quoting an ancient song," he explained. "I have to listen to all this old shit she plays."

"They had hope then. That's why I like it," she replied.

"Doesn't sound very hopeful to me," Bernie muttered.

"Neither does finding your priest," she said.

Fair enough, he thought, and walked away. At least they hadn't asked about his nose.

Bernie took out his vid and called Holland. "No one's seen the priest," he told the captain, "and this won't be sorted out until sometime tomorrow."

"Mobley?"

"It's like a war zone here," Bernie replied. "If he came this direction, I'm betting he took one look and turned right around. I'll keep poking around but it doesn't look good, sir."

"Damn."

"I don't suppose—"

Holland cut him off, anticipating his question. "There's no one by the name of Esmeralda in Walsh's department," he said.

"I'd know her if I saw her again."

"That's all good and fine, but I don't think old Lew would allow us to line inspect his female officers. Besides, I'm betting she was brought in from the outside. Slip in the ranks, do her job, and disappear. So on that note, you might want to hope you don't see her again."

"Yes, sir."

"And for crying out loud, Bernie, don't be so hard on yourself." Holland cut the connection.

Bernie pocketed the vid. For a moment he stared at the madness that surrounded him. The flames were losing their battle, no longer burning so high into the night. But he still heard Satan laughing.

And he sounded like Leonard Litz.

31

Isabelle Bishop wasn't often surprised. However, when her personal assistant announced her latest visitor, she couldn't stop her hand from covering her mouth or catch the muffled hitch in her breathing.

"Give me a couple of minutes and then show her in," she responded.

After her personal assistant left, Isabelle touched her heart while assuring herself it was inevitable. Sooner or later she was bound to appear. Isabelle was important now; it was astonishing it hadn't happened earlier. She set her pen down.

Her study was small, but after marrying J. Henry it became her place of escape, a sort of planning center where she could ground herself in this brave new world of power and political subtleties. He found her letter writing peculiar, unable to understand why she enjoyed the tactile sensation of putting pen to paper in this age of technology. For the longest time, she jested that she would resurrect the lost art of letter writing once she became first lady. Given the recent turn of events, it no longer seemed like such a far-fetched joke.

Isabelle turned over the note she'd been working on. It was addressed to the speaker's wife, a rather sour, disagreeable old biddy but someone worth cultivating. Despite the prevailing bias against handwritten notes, they worked. Isabelle had discovered a simple yet unique way to distinguish herself.

The door opened and her PA escorted in a young woman wearing robes. She was tall and willowy with olive skin and dark eyes. Her hair was bobbed short. She wore no makeup. Isabelle waited for her PA to leave then stood.

"Dear sister," she said, stepping from behind her desk. "What do I owe the pleasure?" She kissed Maria Ashley on the cheek.

"Why haven't you responded to my requests?"

"My dear, I've been very busy. Surely even you've heard the news about J. Henry." She forced a smile, adding, "Please sit down," and pointed to a Queen Anne's chair in front of the desk.

"Oh, yes, I've heard." Maria Ashley took the chair, resting her hands in her lap. "I suppose congratulations are in order."

Isabelle skipped over her sister's insincerity by responding, "It all happened so fast I'm just starting to believe it, too. Such a great responsibility."

"I can see that, but I'm surprised he's willing to place you in harm's way."

Isabelle narrowed her eyes. Maria Ashley had always been bookish, intelligent, and naively idealistic, but hardly savvy. And that last statement had been shrewd, as if laying the groundwork for the true purpose of her visit. She guessed anyone could change. "Whatever do you mean?" she asked.

"Oh, Isabelle, you know perfectly well. Mother always called you her wild child. I remember coming to your aid a couple of times myself. Do you recall that time in the French Quarter?" she started to ask then stopped when her eyes met her sister's stony stare.

"I remember nothing of the sort," Isabelle told her. Next it would be how Maria Ashley held her hand in a Mexican clinic as Isabelle attempted to correct a mistake, the ghost of which she'd buried deep in her memory and paved over with the present. She refused to allow it to haunt her now, especially from her shy, soft-spoken, perfect sister.

"Wait, you don't think—?"

"I don't know what to think."

Her high voice kicked up a notch. "Isabelle, admittedly I came to tell you something, but I certainly didn't mean to imply anything."

"Oh? And what are you afraid you're implying?"

"This isn't going the way I thought it would," she said seemingly to herself. "I don't want to see you hurt."

"There, you've made you intents clear," Isabelle pressed. "I give you whatever it is that you want and I won't get hurt. Some people would call that blackmail, darling."

"I'm not here to blackmail you," Maria Ashley protested. "Have you become so paranoid?"

Isabelle leaned forward. "What do you want from me?"

America Unbalanced

Maria Ashley stood. "Nothing. Not now."

"Don't be a fool. You've gone this far. Say it."

"You misunderstand. I've come to tell you that I'm leaving. All I want is your blessing."

For the second time on this early morning, Isabelle was astonished. Finally, unable to help herself, she began laughing. "My blessing? What on earth for?"

Flustered no doubt by the outburst, Maria Ashley's face reddened. "I plan to take my vows," she replied with an edge of defiance.

"Well, I don't know why you need my blessing for that," Isabelle told her. "If you wish to hideout in some nunnery that's your business."

"I'm not going to hide out in some nunnery, Isabelle. My work calls me to the growing area we've started to call the Wasteland. You know it, of course, as the New Dust Bowl."

"Don't be an idiot. Only criminals and madmen live out there."

"And the poor, infirmed, and spiritually destitute."

Isabelle waved a hand as if swatting a fly. "There's plenty of that in your own backyard. You don't need to travel to Calcutta to find it."

"That is true, and I'll confess that has been part of my struggle."

"Then why leave?"

"Because it's right for me. There are people here already doing good work. Very few have ventured back out into the Barrens, the desert." She glanced up and drew a deep breath.

"At any rate, as you said earlier," Maria Ashley continued, "given the recent turn of events and your new position, I felt I should tell you in person. I'm sure the press would find it newsworthy, even GNN. I didn't want you to be caught unaware."

Isabelle stared at her sister. Maria Ashley's hands were pressed together just below her chin as if any moment now she'd bow and excuse herself. They'd been close once, long ago, before their interests had taken them down paths widely divergent. And for a second Isabelle felt worried, even afraid for her. "Reconsider, Maria Ashley," she said and stood. "Give it a little longer. Times are bad now, but there is hope. People such as J. Henry are working to make things better. I can't explain how because frankly I don't understand it all, but I can tell you this: when change happens, it'll happen fast."

"Your concern is touching, but I've made my decision."

"You'll die out there."

"And you could die here. Not all the criminals and madmen live in the Wasteland."

"You broke Mother's heart when you went off to study with those nuns. If she were alive today, what would she say to this?"

"Indeed, Isabelle, what would she? Don't speak to me of breaking her heart."

So righteous, so righteous, Isabelle thought, and any sympathy she'd felt a moment ago melted from her heart. "Very well, you want my blessing, you have my blessing." She made the sign of the cross.

"Now you mock me."

"I'm angry."

"Please don't be angry, Isabelle. Find it in your heart to be happy for me."

"I can't. But thank you for letting me know. You're right about one thing, the press will have a field day."

A slight smile touched the corners of Maria Ashley's mouth. "You can tell them I was the wild child. Ironic, isn't it?"

"Good bye, Maria Ashley."

"Good bye, Isabelle."

Her sister turned and left. Isabelle sat back down and picked up her pen. Suddenly, her letter to the speaker's wife seemed ridiculous. Then again, she was a ridiculous woman.

Isabelle got back to the work at hand and completed the correspondence.

32

"The food riots in the southwest sector have grown worse," Senator Leonard Litz, hollered to a raucous crowd in Milwaukee, Wisconsin. "You've got to ask yourself, are you next? What happens here when drinking water dries up, like it has down in Houston, in Dallas, in San Antonio, and crops begin to fail? What do you do when there's not enough hothouse production and food grows scarce? I tell you what you do. You go hungry and you riot, just like they are in the southwest. Riot. And people get hurt, killed even, all because there's not enough food.

"You know the food industry's controlled by Wall Street, don't you? Big donors to President Webster are making big bucks off your hungry stomachs. It's the old law of supply and demand, my friends. Only those who can't meet the demands are starving.

"Well, I don't intend to sit around and let that happen. Not like the current administration. We're going to shield our cities against the sun. I tell you we have the technology to do it, but Webster won't lift a finger or spend a dime to help. And we're going to make the desalination industry solid so no one will go without anything as basic as water. Clean, safe, affordable water. I'm going to form a Water Cartel and fill it with security so our water supply is protected and no one will ever go thirsty again.

"In fact, right now, and with the help of my new running mate, J. Henry Bishop, we're working on a bill to fund the southwest desalination plant to help those folks. I might add this is a bipartisan effort. Some members of Webster's own party have joined in, and yet the president has threatened to veto the bill, accusing me of making money off the measure. No proof, just an absurd accusation. I tell you, the man's got to go. He's got to go.

He's pocketing money left and right from bigwigs on Wall Street and he says I'm taking advantage of taxpayers. That's outrageous! I think the old head doctors call that projection, don't you? He's trying to pin his faults and weaknesses on me. And he is a weak man, Weak Webster, that's for sure. It's the old sleight of hand, redirection trick. Oldest trick in the book. Maybe Webster thinks he's a magician, huh? Only it won't work and you know why? Because he's a really bad magician like he's a really bad president. The American people are smart enough to see right through you Weak Webster. So sad. . . ."

33

Bear found the church in ruins.

Squatters had set up shabby lean-tos in the busted lot. Old men, women, and children combed the rubble, desperate for anything worth taking. The rectory had burned almost to the ground. The cathedral looked like a child's doll house after a Doberman had gotten hold of it. Walls had been ripped apart by the muscles of flames, and jagged edges scraped the skyline. Stained glass salted the street with its sacred colors. And beyond the fragments that remained there lurked nothing but darkness.

By God, Bear thought, is this what a life of goodwill now fetches?

Slowly, he pushed his speeder through the depredation. Greedy eyes captured the machine in the glory of their minds. Until their looks caught sight of its driver. They then quickly retreated, searching for easier targets. Bear eased to a stop at the rear of what had been the offices and food pantry and dismounted the speeder.

A blink of an eye ago he'd been upsetting the apple cart. Now he couldn't help but stand in the same place and shoulder some of the responsibility for the desolation that surrounded him. That wasn't to say that the hallowed compound wouldn't have met the same fate. But delivering the shipment of hijacked food had surely accelerated its demise.

Bear secured the speeder and walked around, asking if anyone had seen Father Bartholomew or knew where he was. Most people refused to speak with him, or if they did answer it was with a short shake of the head and averted eyes. He was about to give up when a familiar face appeared before him.

"So you come back to inspect your handiwork," the young woman said.

"That's harsh, love."

Hands out, a short shrug. "Well, as you can see, it's a harsh world," Rachel responded.

"How did it happen?" Bear asked.

"Ugly rumors started by a bunch of thugs. They whipped the masses into a frenzy and then let the dark side of nature take its course." She stared up at him, although Bear saw more of his reflection than of her eyes in her UV glasses. "I haven't eaten all day," she told him.

"Do you know where Father Bartholomew is?"

"I haven't eaten all day," she repeated.

Bear paused. He liked the girl well enough and didn't mind feeding her, but he didn't like to be strung along, or to have the sense she felt entitled. And after all, she survived by manipulating, making her hard to read. "How is it that a girl like you has gone hungry?"

"Funny how when riots break out some men think they can take whatever they want. I've been keeping a low profile. The only reason I came out this afternoon is because I'm hungry. She says for the third time," Rachel added with a twisted grin, and drew close to him. "I'm willing to pay."

"I told you before, love—"

The diminutive girl leaned into him, stood on her tiptoes, and drew as close to his ear as she possible could. "No, you idiot," she whispered harshly, "with information. Now make like you're picking me up and let's get the hell out of here."

"Marvelous," Bear mumbled. He kissed the top of her head, swooped her up and put her on the back of the speeder, unlocked it, and they cruised from the ruins of the gutted church and into a poor neighborhood where even the houses appeared worried.

She had him stop at a taco stand, which was hardly what he'd expected when she said she'd not eaten. At his inquisitive countenance she said, "They don't use dog and get their *masa* and *frijoles* from Mexico so they almost never run out."

"Good to know." Bear figured he got off easy, until he saw the amount of food she stocked up on and realized quantity made up for the bargain prices.

Finally, they cruised to a halt outside a house that once upon a time had been a fine Victorian, probably for a wealthy family. Age and neglect had stripped its paint to flecks and half of the wrap-around porch was missing. Despite the heat, the windows were wide open and shreds of curtains hung in the still air like knotted spider's webs.

"There's no place like home," Rachel stated. She clutched the sack of food as if it was filled with gold coins.

Bear removed his dark glasses and raised an eyebrow.

"We're left alone," she added.

He doubted that was true for anyone, nowadays, but would've thought nothing more of it except that, for a split second, he had a vision, a melding of past, present, and future. First the future as a line of glass and steel buildings flashed in front of his eyes. Clean walkways and crisp patches of well-manicured green edged the edifices. And then the gentrification gradually morphed backward in time, and Bear spotted a boy, maybe nine or ten, running out of the suddenly impressive house, a screen door slamming closed behind him. The boy held a .22 rifle, and a dog followed him as he ran off to the west, a gentle sun in his face, and a field of tall grass before him. Rabbit hunting. On the outskirts of a city not yet a city and the child is going to hunt rabbits. Amazing, he thought.

"Are you all right?" Rachel asked and broke his trance.

He explained to very few people how he could sometimes see things, and this wasn't the time to add to the list. He said, "There were better days, love. Indeed, they were better." Better than now, and better than the sterile ones to come, he realized. What most people didn't understand was that whenever you painted a rosy picture of the past you drained the color from the present. Politicians used the good old days as an opiate when it was nothing more than a placebo.

Rachel sighed. "People say you're a madman."

"Because I'm English?"

She stared at him.

"Probably say I'm a killer and thief, too," he added.

Her eyes widened.

Bear laughed. "Don't worry, love. It's all true."

"Marvelous," she muttered, which only caused him to laugh louder.

Bear followed her up a slab of steps and into the musty house. Instinctively, his hand hovered near his cutter. A distrust of the area more than a distrust of the girl, or so he told himself.

Inside it was dim with ceiling fans pushing the hot air. Bear noticed a staircase to the left but Rachel turned right and set the sack of tacos down on a chipped table in a small sitting room in front. The remnants of a cheap chandelier hung above the table. There was a ratty couch and matching chair, the golden floral pattern long gone to seed, and between them a standing lamp with a lampshade adorned with faded red tassels.

"Wait here," she told him and went toward the back of the house.

Well, she must trust me, he thought. She left the food.

The floor creaked beneath Bear's weight as he poked his head from the front room to a room that in its heyday must've been used for formal dining. Now it was barren with only a few mattresses strewn across the threadbare carpet.

Bear slipped back into the sitting room and waited. He had to admit, the smell of the food stirred his appetite. Soon voices accompanied Rachel's return. They were, as he'd imagined, co-workers. An Asian girl, an African-American, another white, and an Hispanic. All appeared twenty-something, though a couple of the girls may have been older. Bear nodded politely at the introductions, understanding now why they had purchased so many tacos.

The women dug into the food as if they hadn't eaten in a month. Bear held back, but Rachel tossed him a couple of soft tacos. He found them to be mostly rice and beans wrapped in corn tortillas with the occasional prize of meat (not dog, he reminded himself, if the girl could be believed).

"Well, who's going to pay him?" the Asian woman asked as she finished eating.

Before Bear could respond, Rachel said, "I am, of course." She glanced into the sack of tacos, saw a few remaining, and picked it up.

"Oooh," the girls hooted, ignoring Bear's protests.

"Look," the African-American added, "she wants to keep his energy up."

"That not all she wants to keep up," said the Hispanic.

"Really, love," he said, but Rachel simply took his hand and tugged. He resisted once and then twice but her persistence and the ladies' taunts broke him down, and he followed her out of the sitting room, into the hall, and up the creaky stairs.

It was even more stuffy and musty on the second floor. Rachel let go of his hand and beckoned him down the hall to a closed door near the rear of the house.

"You're going to extremes to keep up appearances," he told her.

"You never know who's watching, or who'll sell her soul for another meal." She knocked softly three times then opened the door. The room was small with wooden floors. Another ceiling fan slapped the heat, though with a pair of windows open it was bearable.

A man sat at a small desk, books in front of him, pen and paper close at hand. Rachel tossed the extra tacos next to his work. The man looked up.

America Unbalanced

"I'll be damned," Bear murmured.

It was Father Bartholomew.

34

Holland Copeland had a hunch. Problem was, it involved Lew Walsh. In particular, his cooperation, which he'd never had, even going back to their academy days.

If Holland ran the department, Walsh would've been kicked off the force ages ago. Let him work as a rent-a-cop. Work he was suited for.

Come to think of it, Holland pondered as he drove, ole Lew was already a borderline rent-a-cop, selling himself to the highest bidder. He'd never been able to prove it. As he'd told Bernie Hawke, Walsh was slick. So Holland had waited, and watched, anticipating that eventually the dirty cop would slip up. But it hadn't happened. And Holland had begun to believe it never would.

So if you can't beat 'em, join 'em? Not exactly. More like if you can't beat 'em, use 'em.

Holland didn't intend to confront Walsh at his office. Instead he waited until Lew was off-duty.

Walsh lived in an apartment near the university in a low rent neighborhood filled with college kids and dope dealers. He'd once been married but his wife had run off with a Texas Ranger. Holland figured had it been anyone else, Walsh would've shot him, but he was too afraid to mess with a Ranger. Smart woman on many levels.

Holland parked in front of a dirty brick building. Any semblance of lawn had been beaten to hard packed dirt. Once there'd been a security door and a line of buzzers keeping people from just walking in, but the door was missing and the buzzers were rusted to the side of the building.

America Unbalanced

The hall smelled of stale beer and urine. Holland heard music, vids playing much too loud, and the voices of a couple arguing. Then the power in the apartment complex went down and it became eerily quiet. Even the quarreling couple fell silent.

With no windows and sketchy emergency lights a spidery darkness descended. He paused a moment, allowing his eyes to adjust, before climbing a couple of flights of stairs. Turning down the dim hallway he almost bumped into a young Hispanic woman. Her hair was pulled back into a ponytail, and she wore a black leather jacket, black boots and jeans, making her all that much harder to see.

"Pardon me," Holland said. "Not much light here."

"No harm," she replied and kept going.

Perhaps a college kid, he thought. Who else is going to wear a leather jacket in this heat except some image conscious artist, musician or writer? He came to Walsh's door and was about to knock when he realized it wasn't closed all the way. Holland pulled out his cutter and listened. Murmuring voices surrounded him, but they came from other apartments. After a few seconds he rapped the door with his left hand and called, "Lew? You home? It's Holland."

No response.

He pushed the door open.

The apartment was as messy as Walsh's soul. Food containers and empty booze bottles littered a coffee table in front of a large vid screen. Clumps of clothes covered the floor and a couch even frat boys would probably have rejected.

"Lew?" Holland repeated.

The sole window was in the tiny kitchen. A soiled, half-drawn shade allowed in enough light for Holland to see the dirty plates and mugs in the sink and an army of rocks glasses on the sparse counter space. Frankly, he was surprised Walsh used rocks glasses and didn't just drink straight from the bottle.

Judging from the dead soldiers, Holland expected to see Walsh passed out. There were only two other rooms in the apartment, a small bath and the bedroom. Both doors were open. Walsh hadn't fallen asleep on the throne, thank goodness. Holland found him face down on the bed.

The other window in the apartment was in the bedroom. The shade was completely drawn. Holland raised it as he attempted to rouse Walsh. Glancing out he saw it faced the front of the building. He also noticed the young woman he'd almost bumped into get into a hovercraft and drive away. Nice machine, he thought. Must come from money.

When he turned back to Walsh, Holland recognized his mistake. Lew Walsh hadn't passed out. He had a tidy hole in the back of his head. Blood had seeped onto his pillow and blankets.

Holland rushed back to the window, but the young woman was gone. It had to be, he thought. The hit woman who Bernie had the run in with. What was her name? Esme. Damn.

He pulled out his vid and called it in, describing the woman and hovercraft as best as he could. A dead cop, even a crooked one, would provoke a massive manhunt.

"Well, Lew, you never were very cooperative," he said aloud, studying the dead man. He still had his shoes on. And his shoulder holster, though the cutter was missing. "She was here when you got home, wasn't she, Lew? She was waiting for you."

Holland lifted the dead man's wallet from his back pocket. It held the usual vid credit-chips, driver's license, a little cash, and a business card. Lieutenant Lew Walsh, HPD, and his direct line. On the back of one of the cards was a handwritten number.

From the distance came the sound of sirens. Gradually, they grew louder.

The number might be nothing. Then again the card might disappear. Holland pocketed it. He folded the wallet and set it on the nightstand. He heard the first responders come to a stop below.

Strangely, the power came back on, and the building seemed to come to life again. He glanced at Lew Walsh.

Well, almost to life.

35

Isabelle Bishop found it hard to concentrate. She told herself it was because she was tired. In the waning days of the election, she'd joined the campaign trail. Senator Litz thought she should introduce herself to the public. J. Henry had agreed, and they'd arranged events for her to attend. They were so-called safe affairs—ladies' teas, supporters' luncheons, fund raisers—meant to get her name and face out there and garner some publicity from the press, but not situations where she'd face any real controversy. Still, it was exhausting.

She liked to end the day writing letters. Tonight she sat at a small, round table with a single light shining off the glassy surface. The curtains to the balcony were drawn closed. Isabelle had to think a moment to remember she was in Columbus, Ohio. Madison, Wisconsin had been last night. So many hotel rooms looked the same. Uniformity was meant to instill comfort, dulling the anxiety that the change of traveling created. Isabelle found it the opposite, boring and dulling her interest in local flavor.

Her vid went off, and she saw that J. Henry was trying to reach her. She answered, his image appearing before her.

"Hello, darling."

"Hello, Isabelle. How did the fund raiser go?"

"More money in the war chest, dear. A nice haul, I'm told."

"Very good. The senator's convinced you can soothe the savage beast."

"You make me sound like a snake charmer," she said, pointing her pen at him.

"In the world of politics, that's not a bad thing," he jested.

"Well, I don't want to be a snake charmer. There are already too many serpents in the garden. I'd never have a moment's peace."

J. Henry laughed.

Isabelle set the pen on the table. "And you?"

"I fear I'm beginning to like the role of hatchet man too much," he replied.

"Oh, darling, I wouldn't worry. You'll always be the happy warrior." She forced a smile.

"You look tired, Isabelle."

She was touched by his concern. "I'm not the seasoned politico. I'm afraid I'm letting you down."

"You're fishing, Isabelle," he chided. "Or there's something you're not telling me."

Seeing her opening, she took it, beginning with a sigh. "Before I left Washington, I had a disturbing conversation with my sister."

"Really?" he responded. "Did Maria Ashley tell you she was taking her vows?"

"Why yes. How did you know?"

"I figured it was only a matter of time," he told her. "Frankly, I don't see why it should bother you."

"She left the city. She's going out to the badlands. I think she has delusions of sainthood."

"I see."

"Do you?"

"You're afraid for her."

"The growing New Dust Bowl is turning into a place of murderers and crazy people. And there's a rumor that Litz wants to turn it into a penal area."

J. Henry waved a hand. "Don't believe it. I think the second part of that rumor is that he intends to send his political opponents there. Won't happen."

Isabelle wondered if he was toeing the company line in case their conversation was hacked, or if he really believed Litz was just another man who wanted to be president. Litz meant to disrupt the status quo, upset the apple cart. In short, he wanted his name prominently in the history books.

"Are you asking me to do something?" J. Henry asked. "I can't stop her from going."

"Aren't you afraid of what the press will say?"

"Bah! There might be a mild interest but it'll pass. I return to my original premise. You're afraid for her."

There was much about Isabelle's past that J. Henry didn't know, and she meant to keep it that way. Maria Ashley had rattled the keys to the deepest secrets Isabelle kept locked away, a reminder that the past could be glimpsed at any moment by a keen eye in the present. Because of this, Isabelle anticipated damage control and decided it might be best if her sister was out of sight and thus out of the public mind. Things might come up, but without Maria Ashley around to corroborate them any charge would appear more like an ugly slur by a disgruntled opponent, spurring J. Henry to her defense. Or so Isabelle hoped.

"Perhaps I am worried about her. She is my sister. Do you think we could at least supply her with some provisions and maybe an escort through the Barrens?" she asked her husband.

"So Marie Ashley has gone to the southwest sector?"

"Yes."

"It's pretty volatile down there. Recently a mob burned down a church."

"All the more reason to do anything we can."

"Now the press *would* have a field day if they found out Maria Ashley was receiving special treatment because she's my sister-in-law."

"If you think it's too risky—"

"I didn't say I couldn't or wouldn't help her," he interrupted. "We just need to do it quietly."

"Oh, thank you, J. Henry."

"Of course, dear."

They talked a while longer before disconnecting. It was late, but she seemed less tired, now. In fact she felt energized. Isabelle picked up her pen and tapped the end against the stationary. God help Maria Ashley, she thought. Though if He didn't, they would. They'd help transport her to where she wants to be. It's her choice, Isabelle repeated like a mantra. It's her choice. If Maria Ashley wants to disappear into the lion's den, so be it.

And the sooner the better.

36

Rex Fielder tented his fingers. It appeared Hank Mobley was more resourceful than he'd originally thought.

A jazz band tapped out a mellow tune, brushes on the drums. Fielder had insisted on the same dive where he and Walsh had met. Somehow it seemed appropriate.

A young woman in a black leather jacket entered the bar. She pushed up her dark glasses so they rested on her black hair. Fielder waited until she spotted him. She showed no emotion as she approached, or when he motioned to the chair on the opposite side of the table. She sat.

"People are smoking," she said.

A thin smile touched Fielder's lips. "Let them enjoy it while they can."

A waitress appeared at their table. "Another of these," Fielder told her, pointing to his own glass. She nodded and left.

"You didn't even ask me," the woman said.

"It doesn't matter. It's all terrible."

"Did you see the news?"

"Naturally. Your description is all over the wires. Rather unprofessional, Esme my dear."

"Power had gone down in the building. I didn't see him very well. I thought he was just another loser going to his shithole apartment."

"He's captain to the officer who interrupted your assignment with Mobley."

"Special Forces. Can't you do something about them?"

"I'm working on it," Fielder told her. "In the meantime, what about Mobley?"

The waitress returned and placed a drink from her tray full of drinks on the table. Esme waited until she continued on her rounds before responding. "He's gone underground. With his connections, he could be a thousand miles from here."

"Or right under our noses."

"Either way," the woman said, "the trail's cold." She picked up the drink, sniffed it, and then gave a slight shrug before taking a taste.

"You're braver than I thought," Fielder told her.

"I've had worse." She met his eyes. "Should I disappear before I, ah, disappear?"

"Interesting you should ask. You trust me to give you an honest answer?"

Esme drank again. "I figure blood carries some weight, uncle."

His wolf's jaw jutted out. "Oh, if your mother could see you now."

"She'd probably kill us both. Well?"

Fielder turned his drink one way and another, bottom scraping the table. It was as if he twisted the dial on an old combination lock. "Finish the job with Mobley. Then go away for a while."

"I told you he's faded into the underground."

"Look for a weapon's runner, a large black man with an English accent. I'm betting Mobley wants out of the city. But he'll need someplace to hole up. A Scrap compound. One of those growing religious camps. Something like that."

She appeared skeptical, though she asked, "Where do I find this weapon's runner?"

"My sources say he's back in the city. Somehow he's connected to that church that burned. Start there."

Esme finished her drink and stood. "Very well. Goodbye, uncle."

Fielder nodded like an old gentleman. "I look forward to hearing from you soon. Oh, and niece," he added before she could turn away. "I've been doing my homework. Be very careful of this man. In many ways, he's the opposite of Walsh. And I suspect he'd put the Special Forces cops to shame as well."

"Next you're going to tell me he's the reincarnation of Alexander the Great."

He let her jab at his beliefs roll off his shoulders. His wolfish grin widened. Someday she'd understand. "Or Genghis Khan," he replied. "Be careful, niece."

37

Bear stroked his beard. What the good Father wanted to do went against his instincts, right down to the bone.

"I had to leave quickly," Bartholomew explained. "There wasn't any time to collect them."

The priest didn't understand how lucky he'd been, Bear thought. First, he'd escaped a mob. Second, he'd found sanctuary, albeit in a house of ill repute, yet it was simply because a young hooker liked him. Of course, having bestowed her with food earlier hadn't hurt. You never know the road a favor will pave.

"I believe in karma," Rachel had told Bear as he'd filled the doorway, staring dumbfounded at the priest.

"God works in mysterious ways," Bartholomew had added.

Perhaps he had a point. For the single purpose of playing wagon master to a group of religious misfits, Bear had returned to the city. Again, it went against his better judgment, his creed for survival, but he seemed unable to stop himself.

He had offered the opportunity to live in desolation, to scratch out a new life on the fringe of Hell, to Rachel. She'd laughed.

"I'll stick to the Hell I know," she'd said. "A girl like me wouldn't last long out there."

"You may be surprised."

"You had your chance, big guy."

Bear had let that go. Last thing he needed was a concubine, though of course that hadn't been his intention. Given the current situation, he didn't see a long life for her in the city. But that was her choice.

He focused on the task at hand.

Bear waited until dark before taking Bartholomew back to the church. Small fires dotted the lot as the homeless warmed tins of thin broth made from potato peels or whatever food scraps Bear imagined they could find. He was surprised the authorities allowed these Webstervilles, as the media now called them, to exist. Once more he guessed it was only a matter of time before the storm troopers swooped in and scrubbed these blemishes from the face of the city as they had the Hoovervilles generations ago during the Great Depression.

"Where do you keep your hovercraft?" Bear asked the priest. As clunky as the machine was, it was better than walking.

"On the north side of the rectory. But I suspect it was damaged pretty severely during the riot. We couldn't reach it, which is why we fled on foot." Bear knew that in addition to himself, Bartholomew meant Carlos and Gabe, though where the young Hispanic men were now was anyone's guess.

Bear was beginning to believe that Bartholomew would be his only traveling companion. If so, they could double-up on the speeder and hit the trail. It wouldn't be too hard then to find those greenhorn Brothers, drop Bartholomew off, and let them wander off to start their very own utopia.

No such luck.

"What it is with your precious vids?" Bear asked the Father. He intended to take the opportunity to look at the hovercraft, if only to fulfill his own curiosity.

"It's my personal collection, and it contains all the major religious and philosophical writings of the world, including some that have vanished from the public eye."

"Do you really believe you're the only person with such a compilation?"

"My friend, if we always depend on the other guy to pick up the slack, the noose around our collective necks will surely cut off the air of freedom. It's my duty."

Bear had parked the speeder in the shadows near the damaged hovercraft. "They very well may have been destroyed by the bloody mob."

"The library, yes. But I keep the rare vids locked away."

Bear secured the speeder. Bad vibes rose from the ruins like creatures from Hell lurking on the edge of sanity. He glanced at the hovercraft but realized he couldn't send the priest in alone. Yellow warning tape, a quaint attempt by the authorities to keep people out, lay ripped and on the ground.

America Unbalanced

Bear walked the priest into the destruction. Gaping holes in the roof let in the night sky. It wasn't enough to blow away the smell of soot, burned plastic, and charred dreams. The rectory was a shell of what it'd been. A couple of vagrants emerged from the darkness but retreated swiftly when they spotted the cutter the big man brandished.

"Judging from the shambles," he told Bartholomew, "I highly doubt the vids survived."

"Have a little faith, Bear. Literature is amazingly durable."

Father Bartholomew bore a devilish expression as he entered the area that had been his living quarters. At first glance anything worth taking seemed taken. The priest ran his hand down a patch of wall until he found what he wanted. It took a little effort but he managed to unlatch a section and fold it down like a shelf. Tucked in the shelf was a slender box, and inside the box a line of vids.

"I enjoy reading each night before sleep," he explained.

"Marvelous. But how did you know it hadn't gone up in flames?"

"I invested in this box years ago. It's made from the same alloy as the new transports. Strong as an ox, light as a feather. Remarkable material, don't you think?"

"Why yes." Chasing the vagrants away hadn't chased away his bad feeling. "You have them, now let's go."

"By all means."

As they emerged into the sparse city light, a sickle of moon above them, another figure stirred. Bear leveled his cutter.

"Don't shoot! Don't shoot!" a man said. "Bear, it's me. Hank Mobley."

"Mobley?" He didn't lower the cutter. "What in the devil are you doing here?"

"Looking for the priest. Well, looking for the priest in order to find you."

"Come over where I can see you."

Mobley stepped into a dull patch of white light, hands held up. "I have a cutter, but I didn't draw it." When the big man said nothing, he added, "They tried to kill me."

"Who tried to kill you?"

"You've got to get me out of here. I'd leave the country but it's as hard getting out as it is getting in these days. Bear, I'm begging you. I'll even hide out in the Wasteland if I have to."

"You didn't answer my question."

"I can't."

"Why? You afraid they'll kill you if you tell me?"

"Just get me out of here, Bear. Then I'll tell you whatever you want to know."

Bear didn't trust him. "How do I know you're not the cheese in a trap for me?"

"I swear it's not a trap. They tried to kill me," he repeated. "They sent a hit man after me. Well, a woman, actually, and it would've worked if a Special Forces cop hadn't stumbled in. The whole thing's about to blow, or that's what some very powerful people are afraid of."

Bear felt Father Bartholomew touch his shoulder. "This isn't the time for compassion, Padre. I know this man."

Mobley dropped to his knees. He was practically in tears. "You're sentencing me to death."

"His fear is genuine," the priest whispered.

"I've seen many fine actors in my time," he replied. Bear went over and put the end of the cutter to Mobley's head. "Give me a name."

"You don't want it. You'll be a dead man, too."

"I've been a dead man for decades."

"I can get you a transport," Mobley said. He motioned toward the priest's hovercraft. "That thing will never get off the ground. Look at the fire damage."

"How many people do we have going?" Bear asked Bartholomew.

"A half dozen, maybe more."

Bear strongly considered cutting Mobley down. Had the good Father not been with him, the decision would've been easier. Mobley was baggage from a train wreck waiting to happen.

Mobley must have sensed Bear's feelings because he blurted out, "Litz. It's Leonard Litz. He wants chaos. He's been strong-arming the election with his thugs."

And you're one of them, Bear thought, eying him coolly. "You think you're telling me something I don't know, mate?"

Mobley opened his mouth. At first nothing came out, and then he stammered, "B-but how?"

"Radical populism rises on the shoulders of ignorance and the empty promise of impossible dreams," Bartholomew spoke up. "Any student of history can recognize the formula."

Bear took a step back and lowered his cutter. The man had offered validity to Bear's lingering suspicions, but it wasn't enough. "I want proof."

"What good will that do?"

"There are people, even in the crooked media, who want to bring the senator down. Corruption doesn't breed unity."

"What, a transport's not good enough?" he tried to joke. When Bear leaned toward him again, Mobley added, "The warehouse. We need to go back to my warehouse office."

Bear smelled a trap and shook his head. "They'll be watching. And by now they've tossed your office like a cheap salad."

"I can get us in."

"Sorry, mate, I don't trust you."

"They turned on me, Bear. I want to see them go down, including Litz." When the big man didn't respond, he continued, "You could've killed me that day at the warehouse, but you didn't. I owe you. I have names, dates, vid messages, transaction numbers, and they're in a safe spot."

"Like my personal library," Father Bartholomew said gently to Bear. "He may be speaking the truth."

"And behind the warehouse is a compound where I keep my own fleet of hovercrafts."

Bear looked at the priest. "Half a dozen, you say?"

"At the very least."

"How can that be?"

"God works in mysterious ways," Bartholomew replied.

Or He's on vacation and Satan's picking up the slack, Bear thought. He stared hard at Mobley. "If you're lying to me, the last bloody thing I'll do is kill you. Do you understand?"

Mobley nodded vigorously. "Yes, yes, I understand."

Bear slid his cutter into its holster. Mobley stood.

"By the way," the big man asked, "who was the soldier?"

"Soldier?"

"The man at the warehouse in the fatigues. The man, as the saying once went, who threw you under the bus when he pushed you into me."

"Colonel Rex Fielder."

"Army?"

"Special Ops, and a Litz man to the end."

Marvelous, Bear thought. He crossed his arms and studied the damaged hovercraft. Even from here he could see that Mobley was right about one thing. The transport was grounded. What the fire hadn't touched, scavengers had. This just keeps getting better and better. He turned back to Mobley. "You better have a plan," he said, "and I better like it."

38

Morning broke. Holland Copeland addressed his team. "I've been directed to join the manhunt for Lieutenant Walsh's killer. The suspect is a young woman in her mid- twenties, dark hair, dark eyes, approximately five foot six inches tall and weighing maybe a hundred and ten or twenty pounds. Goes by the name of Esmeralda, calls herself Esme, no known last name. I only caught a glimpse of her. Officer Hawke had a better look during his encounter."

"Sounds like someone I wouldn't mind encountering," said Randy Clute, laughing. A couple of the other officers chuckled, too. Holland didn't crack so much as a grin.

"Then you'd probably be dead, Officer Clute," the Captain said. "Don't fool yourselves, gentlemen. She is extremely dangerous. Lew Walsh found that out the hard way.

"We're going to pair up. The deputy commissioner wants us to retrace Walsh's last steps. Patrols are already combing the area around the apartment complex. Gilchrest and Smith, see what you can find out at The Baker Street Cafe. Walsh had an on-again, off-again relationship with the owner and ate breakfast there almost everyday. Hawke and Peterson, you talk to his mother. She's in St. Cecilia's, the nursing home off Shepard. Apparently she took the news hard and no one's spoken with her since. You're both good with people. It's a long shot but we need to talk to her. Clute and I will check out his watering holes, which I heard were many. Any questions?"

No questions, so Holland dismissed them. He'd decided to keep Clute with him. He was such an over-the-top Litz supporter, the captain had begun to wonder if he was a mole, though he wasn't too bright. At the very least, he figured he could shield the other men from Clute's annoyance.

As the meeting dispersed, Holland ordered Clute to pull a hovercraft around and then caught Bernie. "I want a minute with you."

Bernie hovered, and when it was just the two of them in the briefing room, Holland spoke. "The deputy commissioner shared another tidbit of information this morning, but this is between you and me."

"Of course."

"There's going to be a shake-up in the department, and we're part of it." He paced over to a bank of windows and stared out at the bail bondsman's office across the way. "They're breaking up our team, reassigning everyone."

Bernie tensed. "What? They can't do that," he protested.

"They can," Holland replied, turning around, "and they are. It has to do with this new division they're starting that's somehow tied into the Water Cartel. The desalination plants are now considered a national priority, and the upper brass wants a separate department defending them. This is coming all the way from the bigwigs in D.C."

"I thought all this talk was Litz rhetoric."

"It's been in the making for a while now. He's been one of its proponents, so of course he's taking all the credit."

"Well, I don't see what that has to do with us."

"Manpower and money, Bernie. Manpower and money. Listen to Kelly once in a while. She'd tell you the same thing. At any rate, that's what I wanted to talk to you about." Holland retrieved his Stetson from the front of the room. He made like he was molding the crown and adjusting the brim as he half-sat on a table. "I've recommended you for this new Water Cartel division. It would mean a pay raise with the chance for promotion. I hear that Skip Gallagher is going to head it here in the southwest. Skip's a good man. I've known him for years."

"Where are they assigning you?" Bernie asked.

"Don't know yet." He let out a short laugh. "To be honest, Bernie, I'm thinking it might be time for me to retire. I'm not so sure I want to ride in a new rodeo."

"If you don't call it quits, I'd rather stick with you."

"Not my choice." He put his hat on. "You'd be a fool not to take the job with the Water Cartel, if they offer it, which I'm almost certain they will. They need good men, and you're a good man, Bernie. It's going to be a good gig, and with a kid on the way don't tell me you couldn't use a little extra cash." Holland smiled.

"Thank you, sir."

America Unbalanced

"You'd best get going. Your partner's waiting."

"I thought Clute was my partner."

"I'll put up with him today. Consider it my farewell gift." He winked.

Bernie forced a smile.

The hunt began.

39

A barking dog caused Bear to stir. It was hot and muggy, the air still. Weary after only a few hours sleep, he rose.

The house had been buzzing all night. In his shallow dozing, he'd understood that it had attracted people like lost souls to a heavenly floodlight. He made his way downstairs, hoping there was coffee. No such luck. But there was tea, and Bear had a big mug of it. A familiar face met him in the kitchen. It was the young man who'd driven the Father's hovercraft when they'd given the food away.

"They have blocks set up around the city," Carlos told Bear.

"Who has?"

"The army. The police. They say they're looking for a cop killer."

Bear caught sight of Mobley, who was also up, or hadn't gone to bed—no, sleep—because he'd been instantly drawn to the ladies of the house. Cop killer? Bear wasn't so sure. But Carlos was right. They were searching for someone.

Carlos and Gabe had returned, this time with their families. Bear didn't understand why they hadn't laid low in their neighborhood, until he learned that they were being evicted and that soon their homes would be flattened to make room for a fancy new high-rise apartment. Bear understood now. The new order was being built on the bones of the poor. Used to create chaos, once their usefulness was spent, so were they.

The gathering concerned Bear. If word traveled fast among those wanting to leave the city, it would also reach the ears of those who wanted them to stay. Not that leaving the city was prohibited; it was that leaving, and going

117

where they were going, had become dangerous. And the rise of checkpoints didn't ease anyone's anxiety.

The night before, Mobley had recounted the attempt on his life. As Bear extracted the shady businessman from his cast of lovers, he thought it was no wonder they'd sent a woman to take him out, and that it'd almost worked. "Come on, Romeo. We have a job to do."

"Bear, I think I'll stay right here."

"I'll not put these women in harm's way."

"Who's going to look for me here? Besides, they could use someone to organize them."

"How very altruistic of you to volunteer to be their pimp. Let's go."

"You have no right to order me around."

Feeling our oats, are we? Bear thought and stared at him, trying to decide whether to rattle his teeth or rip his arm off.

Mobley gulped. "OK, I'm coming, I'm coming."

Bear went out the front door to wait on the porch. Rachel stepped outside with him. "You have to get these people out of here."

"I'm working on it, love."

"Work faster. I didn't bargain for all this attention."

Bear noticed Bartholomew coming up the walkway, speaking to a young woman in robes. Yet another pilgrim, he thought with a sigh.

"And take Mr. Mobley with you," Rachel added. "He is a disgusting man."

"Yes, he'll fit in well where we're going. Tell the others to be ready. If Mobley's telling the truth, we'll be gone by evening."

Rachel nodded. As soon as Mobley came out the door, she turned and went back inside.

"Not very friendly," he observed.

"You're lucky she doesn't make you a eunuch."

Mobley shuddered.

Bear smirked.

Mobley rode double with him on the speeder. "Stop short of the warehouse," his rider called. "You'll see a Vietnamese restaurant that looks like it's under construction. I own it, and it'll never open. But there's a passage that leads underground that'll take us into the main hanger."

"You don't think it's been discovered?" Bear called.

"You'd have to know it exists in order to find it."

"And the man in the fatigues doesn't know about it?"

"I never told anyone," Mobley stated. "That hole is only for this rabbit."

Hounds have a way of sniffing out their prey, he thought. "And the transport?" Bear asked.

"On the far side of the compound. Again we can reach it underground. But once we get in, we won't have much time. There are vids everywhere."

"Don't worry about the vids," Bear told him.

"What do you mean?"

Bear chose not to explain about the scramblers, nor did he inform him yet that he was donating the transport to Father Bartholomew. Let it be a surprise.

Bear felt Mobley tap him on the side. "Slow down," he directed.

The big man eased off. Soon they came to an old strip mall where a half-assed job of renovation appeared to be underway. Bear glided to a stop beside a skinny live oak tree sprouting from a hole in the walkway. It was more brown than green.

Mobley hopped off. He shooed away a drunk who sat, bottle in hand, snug against the door of the empty storefront. A sign hung announcing that coming soon was the grand opening of The Vietnamese Garden. He keyed a pad, pushed open a pair of doors, and beckoned Bear to drive the speeder inside the building.

Seeing this, the drunk stood up and started to follow. Bear swung off the speeder, pushed up his glasses, and glared at him. Swaying in the doorway, the drunk widened his eyes and then squinted. "I know you," he slurred.

Bear responded by turning to Mobley. "Give the man some money."

"Who carries cash these days?" he asked. "And what makes you think I have any?"

"Most people pack some cash since the power grid's so faulty," Bear replied, "and I know you. Do it."

Grudgingly, he dug out a few bills and handed them to the drunk. Then he slammed and locked the doors. "You're a soft touch with someone else's funds," he grumbled.

"Don't you find it odd he's the only person around?"

"Bums are everywhere."

"Silent witnesses to humanity."

"What does that mean?"

"I wouldn't be surprised if he's been paid to keep an eye out," Bear shot back. "But all he's thinking about right now is another bottle of hooch and food in his belly. Perhaps your rabbit's hole isn't so secret after all, mate." Again Bear had a bad feeling about this. "Oh, and if you have any more cash in your office, you'd better bring it," he added. "Where we're going, credit means nothing."

"If I didn't know any better I'd say you were out to fleece me."

"And if I didn't know any better I'd say you were setting me up."

"Touché." Mobley led Bear though a small dining area, stacks of tables and chairs shove up against a wall, and pushed through the swinging door that opened into the kitchen. There were stainless steel tables, deep sinks, and even a stove. Pretty elaborate for a restaurant that would never open, Bear thought.

"Do you think the bum really knew you?" Mobley asked.

"I can't imagine."

"Maybe this isn't such a good idea."

"Don't go wobbly kneed now, mate."

Mobley pushed aside a rolling rack. Beneath it was a hatch that at first glance could easily be mistaken for a drainage duct. He pulled on the grate and a section of floor swung open. "Well?"

Bear noticed that Mobley had paled, which actually made him feel better. If the shyster was frightened, it was less likely it was a set-up. "Well?" he echoed.

"You sure about this?"

"Lead on, Macduff."

And down the rabbit's hole they went.

40

Holland remembered the card in his back pocket. He took it out and studied the handwritten number on back. So far he'd kept this to himself, not even telling the deputy commissioner he had it. The captain wasn't sure why he hadn't shared the card. It was evidence. Call it a gut feeling.

He pulled out his vid and punched in the number. The screen remained dark, blocked he guessed, but the audio was clear.

"Mitch Skyler Enterprises, Mr. Skyler's office."

Holland didn't miss a beat. "Mitch Skyler, please. This is Captain Holland Copeland, Special Forces Southwest Sector."

"May I ask what this is about?"

"Lieutenant Lew Walsh's murder."

"Oh," the voice squeaked. "Let me see if he's available." She placed him on hold. A generic blurb of classical music played. A flat rendition of Mozart, though he couldn't identify the particular piece. Not that he tried too hard. Instead he was turning Skyler's name over in his mind, trying to recall why it sounded familiar.

The woman came back on the line. "Mr. Skyler's in a meeting and can't speak with you right now."

"Have him get back to me at his earliest convenience," Holland said.

"Yes, sir."

Holland signed off. "Mitch Skyler," he muttered to himself and slipped the card away.

He must've been taking too long for Clute because the officer had come back inside and poked his head into the room. "Ready when you are, Captain."

"Give me a second." He put a call into the deputy commissioner, who was also in a meeting and unavailable. Holland left word he needed to talk to him. It was a good bet Skyler would spark some interest, and maybe by the time the deputy commissioner returned his call Holland would remember who good ole Mitch was.

Once in the hovercraft, the officer asked, "Where to?"

"I want to start at that warehouse where Walsh picked up Mobley."

"I thought we'd been all over it."

That had been Walsh's job, and Holland doubted the lieutenant had done much more than get Mobley out of there. "I'm sure we have," he responded, "but I'd like to poke around some."

"You're the boss." Clute pulled out into traffic and headed for the east side of the city. A call came in that a crowd had formed downtown at Tranquility Park. The dispatcher was asking for units to monitor the situation.

"Too close to city hall for the mayor's comfort," Clute stated.

"You're probably right," Holland agreed.

"They should just send them riot boys in there and bust it up. You know there's going to be trouble."

"People have the right to assemble."

"They ain't assembling. They's just getting ready to start fires, loot businesses and destroy property. Should we swing by there?"

"They don't need us," Holland replied.

"Yes, sir."

Holland knew there was nothing Clute wanted more than to crack a few heads. On the other hand, he'd fit in just as well with the mob that, according to Clute, was getting ready to start fires, loot and vandalize. How Bernie Hawke had put up with him all this time, Holland didn't know. In fact he felt a twinge of guilt at saddling Bernie with Clute. But it all worked out. Bernie would get that job with the Water Cartel, and Skip Gallagher would love him.

As for Holland, the idea of retirement was growing on him. It'd give him more time to raise his chickens and tend the garden. And he could make a little egg money, as his old granny used to say. Only he meant it literally.

Finding Walsh in that cheap apartment with a hole in the back of his head had rattled Holland. Too many old cops were ending their careers with toe tags, and he decided he didn't want to be one of them.

He needed to explain this to Bernie. Holland had seen the look in the young officer's eyes, the look that accused him of getting ready to hunker down in his compound and that'd be the last the world ever saw of old Holland Copeland. Well, there were worse ideas, even if he didn't intend to do it.

But he wasn't retired yet. So in the meantime he needed to track down Lew's killer. Lew had been a cop, and you don't let cops die by the hand of a hired gun. Not even bad cops like Lew Walsh.

Mentally, he ticked off his plan: start at the warehouse, tell the deputy commissioner about Mitch Skyler, and go back to Walsh's apartment.

"There she blows," Clute declared, jarring Holland from his thoughts.

Sure enough, the dispatcher announced trouble had broken out and cops were being diverted to downtown. Responding to Clute's look, Holland shook his head.

"Keep going," the captain stated. "We have our job to do."

"Yes, sir."

Yep, retirement was looking better and better.

41

Holland didn't know he was being tailed. And that made it easy for Esme to keep them in sight.

A young cop and his commander. Too bad it hadn't been the other young cop. Then she'd have both her eggs in the same basket.

Before the call, she'd been faced with a decision. Shadow the officer who'd interrupted her assignment, or follow the commander. Pride taunted her to pick up the cop who'd made her look like a fool. He deserved her undivided attention.

And then she'd heard from her uncle. Some captain from the southwest sector had called Mitch Skyler's office. "Find out what he knows," he'd told her.

"You have a name?"

"Holland Copeland."

She guessed it was just as well. The young cop would be engaged in routine investigation. Her path with him would have to wait for another day. If there were any cards to be played, the old cop would be holding them.

And apparently he was.

She followed the old cop.

42

J. Henry Bishop had flown back to Washington for the vote on the supplemental spending bill for the southwestern desalination project. President Webster had threatened to veto the bill, claiming it would fill the pockets of Litz's cronies. But J. Henry doubted Webster would go through with it, not if he had any hope of holding onto the presidency. Too many jobs were at stake. Too many people were suffering for lack of food and fresh water, both of which the desalination plant would help alleviate.

However, the vote was only one reason for his trip back. He had a promise made to Isabelle to keep.

He'd thought about going to Leonard Litz but decided the senator had enough on his mind without imposing a family matter on him. Instead he called on General Samuel T. Leatherwood. General Sam, as he was commonly called, operated out of the Pentagon. J. Henry had worked with him a couple of years back to help push funding through for the design and development of the First Generation of Unmanned Stealth bombers, or F-GUS as it became known. Production was now underway, pleasing General Sam to no end. The way J. Henry saw it the general owed him one.

General Sam stood as J. Henry entered his office. He was of medium build, not too tall, and his flattop had turned silver, but the general was still fit as a Marine.

"Congressman, it's good to see you."

"You as well." J. Henry met his firm handshake.

"I suppose congratulations are in order for joining the Litz ticket. It's commendable of you for stepping in after the tragedy in Detroit."

America Unbalanced

"Thank you. It wasn't what I'd envisioned for myself at this point. However, sometimes Fate makes you an offer you can't refuse."

The general motioned to a chair and once they both sat, the desk between them, he said, "I've never heard Fate compared to the Godfather before. But I'm sure you didn't come here to talk about ancient films. What do I owe the pleasure of this visit?"

J. Henry cleared his throat and looked around. The office was tidy, an American flag in one corner, and military pictures on the wall, including one of Colonel Theodore Roosevelt when he rode with the Rough Riders. This was going to be harder than he'd thought.

"Let me be frank," he began. "I've come to ask a favor."

"Sounds serious," General Sam replied with a smile.

"To my wife I guess it is."

"OK. I've not had the pleasure of meeting her."

"A situation I'll certainly correct after the election."

"Perhaps at one of the inaugural balls?"

"Absolutely," J. Henry replied. "In the meantime, however, I could use a little help." The general showed little emotion as J. Henry told him about Maria Ashley, her decision to take her vows, and head into the badlands to do her missionary work.

"The long and the short of it," he concluded, "is that we'd like to see that she is escorted safely to wherever she wishes to go. And we plan to send supplies with her. Understand that they'll be coming from my own personal stock."

"So you want me to provide her with an escort," General Sam deduced.

"Yes."

"Why don't you hire an independent service?"

"I need someone who can navigate her and whoever's with her through the checkpoints that have sprouted in the southwest."

General Sam leaned back in his chair. For a moment he was silent. Finally he grinned. "Well," he drawled, "this is highly irregular, but I guess I owe you one for pushing the F-GUS funding through. I'll have a unit ready by the end of the day. Where is she?"

"We've traced her to a questionable neighborhood in Houston."

"I'll be glad when the demolition begins and all that old trash fades like a bad memory."

"Just let me get my sister-in-law out first."

"Not a problem, Congressman Bishop. That won't be a problem at all."

43

Mobley pushed open a trap door on the other side of the tunnel, and Bear followed him up and into the dark warehouse. The air was stifling, musty, the rusty smell of iron and grease lingering in the stillness.

Bear caught Mobley by the elbow. "Electric torches?"

"Come on, we can just turn on the lights."

"Electric torches," Bear insisted.

"I don't get it."

Bear pointed to the narrow upper level windows. "There's no need to signal to the world someone's in here. We disturb as little as possible. In and out."

"Fine." Mobley fumbled his way to a cluster of lockers shoved up against the back wall. It took a couple of tries but he finally found a pair of lights and handed one to Bear. They swept their beams around the cavernous interior, bringing definition to its murkiness. Thick chains hung from overhead booms. An overturned dolly lay in front of a forklift. Scraps of fruit and vegetables crusted the floor. Flies hovered. But for all appearances, they were the only ones in there.

"I'll go up to the office," Mobley said. "It'll take a few minutes to get what you need. While I'm doing that, you take the tunnel to the transport compound, work your magic on the vids, and pull a hovercraft over to the front of the restaurant. I'll meet you there. By the time anyone sees us, we'll be cruising off into the sunset."

Bear hesitated.

"What? I'm not going to run off on you. In and out," Mobley echoed. "And believe me, I'm counting on you to get me out."

"Very well. Don't forget any spare cash you have lying around."

"I haven't forgotten."

An edge had crept into his voice. "Good," Bear shot back. "Because you also need to remember, mate, I'm not doing this out of the goodness of my heart."

"Right now we need each other," Mobley responded, though the edge was gone and it came out weak, almost as if he was pleading. Rather than prolong the conversation, he ran his light over the surface of a workbench until he found a scratch pad and pen. He scribbled a series of numbers down. "The code for deactivating the alarm and opening the gate," he explained.

Bear pocketed the paper. "How long do you need?"

"Fifteen minutes." He paused. "How do I know you won't get what you want and leave me here like you did the last time?"

"We made a deal. Don't insult me."

"OK, OK. Fifteen minutes," he repeated.

"Try to make it ten." Truth be told, the warehouse gave Bear the willies. He didn't know why. He'd certainly been to worst places.

"I'll try," Mobley said, and jogged off toward the stairs that led up to his office.

Whatever information he has, it had better be worth it, Bear thought. He dragged the light across the floor until he found the tunnel. Then once more he dropped into the rabbit's hole, although with each step a heavy feeling grew in the pit of his stomach, weighing him down.

44

Clute stopped the hovercraft in the loading zone of the warehouse. Holland braced himself for the blast of heat that would hit him once he stepped outside. It might be a good distraction. In his mind, he still mulled over his earlier vid conversation, though he wasn't getting anywhere.

"Mitch Skyler," he muttered.

Clute swung his attention to Holland in full force. "What's that, Captain?"

Holland didn't know what startled him more, that he'd spoken aloud without intending to or Clute's strong reaction. "I was thinking of something I'd run across, or rather I should say someone."

"You said Mitch Skyler."

"I did. You know him?"

"Hell no, but anyone who supports Senator Litz knows who he is."

For a second, Holland was speechless. Finally he managed to spit out, "Litz?"

"Sure, Captain. Skyler's one of his advisors. I don't know which one. You know how politicians have advice-givers for all kinds of things. I remember him because his name jumped out at me first time I heard it. Skyler, you know, reach for the sky. I'm surprised you hadn't heard of him."

"Funny but I had. I just couldn't place where." That's what he got for only half-listening to Litz's idiocy.

"So where'd his name come up?" Clute asked.

Holland wasn't willing to share anything with this Litzer. "Oh, I heard his name on some news report and it's been bugging me, like when you can't remember the name of some tune you're humming. So thanks. It's been driving me crazy."

From the way Clute was staring, Holland could tell the young officer didn't believe him. But he had the sense to say, "Glad I could help. Should we go inside?"

"That's what we're here for," Holland replied. But he felt shell-shocked. An advisor to Senator Leonard Litz? For a little man, it suddenly seemed that Lew Walsh was into something very big. Very big, indeed.

45

Esme watched, wondering why the two cops sat so long in their hovercraft. They had to be onto something. Something that warranted a closer look.

She checked her cutter.

She'd parked in front of an empty storefront, eased out of her craft and walked the length of a shabby strip center, stopping when she came to the fringe of an empty lot. Closer to the warehouse was a garbage bin. To get to it, though, would expose her. So she waited, huddled against the corner of the end building.

The short bundle of retail space looked like someone's bad idea of a joke. If she hadn't felt the brick and mortar with her own hands, she'd have thought this was nothing but a facade for a low budget movie.

The sound of shuffling drew her attention from the cops. A vagrant stumbled up to her. He held a bottle and reeked of urine and liquor.

"I know you," he slurred.

"I don't think so," she told him.

He squinted and tried to focus on her. When he realized what she had pointed at him, his eyes went wide.

Esme shot him twice. The old drunk dropped the bottle of whiskey as he fell. It shattered on the concrete. She looked at his body crumpled on the ground and shot him again.

When she turned back to the cops, she saw them leaving their hovercraft. About time, she thought. She waited while the commander keyed a remote and took down the police shield. A crime scene still, so no one else had been there but cops. Still, what was he looking for? Not that it mattered. She had her orders.

Once they were inside the building, she stepped from the shadows and followed.

46

Amazed, Bear faced a fleet of hovercrafts. "That asshole has more bloody money than he let on," he said to the armada. "I think my rates have risen substantially." Some models were so new he half-expected them to answer him back.

He picked a smart looking machine with a reinforced hull that would easily carry a dozen passengers. Interestingly, too, he noticed mounts on both flanks, perfect for a couple of blasters poking out the long, narrow slide windows. In a different age, this would be a rum-runner's dream, he thought.

Mobley's code worked like a charm.

Bear inched the transport out of the compound. He didn't bother securing the gate. They wouldn't be back.

He could attach his speeder to the back, which was what he'd do as he waited. That way he and Mobley could travel together. And it was time to travel. To get the hell out of Dodge, as the old saying went.

But when he pulled around to the restaurant that would never open, he saw another hovercraft. Company.

Bear looked toward the front of the warehouse. Across the way, a police hovercraft stared at him like the evil eye from the floating face of doom.

He jumped out of the transport. Further down the storefront, something caught his eye. Cutter drawn, he approached the body of the drunk. That heavy feeling in the pit of his stomach grew cold. Since leaving Mobley, all hell had broken loose.

America Unbalanced

Then Bear heard the blasts and started to run.

47

Holland spotted Mobley before Mobley saw him. Satchel in hand, he was coming down the stairs from his office, studying his vid as he stepped. How he'd gotten through the police shield, Holland couldn't figure. He drew his cutter and motioned Clute to move to his left so he'd be between the person of interest and the door.

Mobley hit the bottom steps before he realized something was wrong. The glare coming in from the outside door, Holland guessed.

"Well, Mr. Mobley," the captain said, "you are a hard person to catch up to."

Mobley tensed, glancing left then right. "What are you doing here?"

Suddenly, the lights clicked on, chasing away the shadows. Holland peeked over and saw that Clute had found the main switch. "I could ask you the same thing," he answered. "This is a crime scene."

"It's my warehouse. And you have no right to detain me." He started walking toward the door.

Holland cut him off. "I have every right to question you. And I will."

"I have friends."

"According to the last report from one of my officers, that's debatable."

Mobley clutched the satchel to his chest as if he could use it as a shield. "Wait, that cop was with you?"

"Apparently he saved your life. When you meet him, you should thank him."

"I appreciate it, Lieutenant . . ." he let his voice trail off.

"Captain Copeland. But I can understand your confusion, seeing that Lew was a lieutenant. Just how did Lew fit in?"

"Who?"

"Lieutenant Lew Walsh. You knew him. He's the one who whisked you out of here to keep my officer from questioning you. Now I'm guessing that Lew was one of Mitch Skyler's ground troops."

Mobley winced. If the lights hadn't been on, Holland would probably have missed it. Under the brightness, though, it was as clear as the fear on his face.

Clute about spat. "Lieutenant Walsh and Mitch Skyler? That's a boldface lie."

"In your place, officer," Holland warned.

"You don't know what you're getting into," Mobley said.

"Oh, I have a fairly good notion, and you're going to help me prove it."

"You want to take down the senator?" Mobley started to cackle. Its odd echo only added to Holland's unease.

"I intend to uphold the law," Holland replied. "I have no control on where it goes from there."

"The fate of one of the most powerful men in the country in the hands of a tired, old redneck cop. I love it."

"What are you talking about?" Clute asked.

Holland ignored him. "You've had your laugh, Mr. Mobley. Now you're coming with us to the station."

Mobley shook his head. "I don't think so, but I'll do you one better." He reached into the satchel.

Holland leveled his cutter at him.

"I'm not holding a weapon," Mobley stated. "I promise you'll find this very interesting. And I think my partner would approve," he added more to himself than to them.

"Slowly."

Mobley pulled out a small box. "Inside are storage chips with information about every food shipment hijacked in this area. Not only that, there are communiqués, conversations, you name it, linking Walsh and Skyler and a whole lot of other people you don't even know about. I bet with a little police work, you'll get your justice. It might even make you chief.

"So what do you say?" he continued. "I toss you this. You let me walk out that door."

Holland shook his head. "Son, I don't make blind trades."

"You only need to download one chip into your vid and you'll see I'm telling the truth."

"No can do. Besides, you're a witness."

"Then I'm a dead man."

"The senator's right," Clute stammered. "The establishment's trying to throw the election with a shit-pile of lies."

"And don't say you can protect me," Mobley added, his voice skipping up a notch as he turned his attention to Clute.

"Lies!" Clute repeated, raising his cutter.

Holland risked a look at his officer. "Lower your weapon," he ordered.

"The system's rigged because of people like you," the officer told Mobley.

"Clute!"

Mobley backed up the steps as Clute moved closer.

Holland swung his cutter in the officer's direction. Before he could fire, a blast seared the dead air of the warehouse. Clute went down, wide-eyed disbelief lingering in his vacant eyes.

Holland turned back to Mobley, expecting to see a cutter in his hand. But the man continued to clutch the satchel, one hand fisted around the small box.

What the hell? he thought.

48

Esme had briefly debated whether or not she should let the young officer do her job. It would've made the situation easier. The young cop kills Mobley, she kills the young cop, and she'd only have to contend with the old man. But she'd heard enough of the conversation to decide she wanted Mobley alive. For now. She had to find out what he knew. She needed to see what was on those chips.

But first the old man.

She fired another blast from the open door. It sparked off one of the dangling chains. The old cop ducked and rolled, coming up on one knee. He returned fire.

Holding the cutter with both hands, she crouched low, back against the outside of the building, then swung around and shot again.

The old man fired back but his blasts sailed high.

She had him in her sights and squeezed. The commander went down.

Searching for Mobley, she saw him scrambling toward the back of the warehouse. She cut him in the back of the leg. He yelped, dropped the small box, and clutched his hamstring. She shot him in the other leg, and he yelped again. Still gripping the satchel, he went down face first.

The old man groaned, trying to reach for the cutter he'd lost. Calmly, Esme walked over and kicked him in the face and then kicked the cutter so it skidded across the warehouse surface.

Propped on his elbows, Mobley tried to drag himself away. He managed inches at a time. Esme smirked as she approached him.

Mobley stopped. His breathing was heavy. Leaning on his left elbow, he twisted slightly to look up at her. "I didn't expect to see you again."

"And that's your mistake."

"It's hard to fight pure dumb luck."

She almost smiled. "Now you know how I felt the first time."

Eyes filled with desperation, he said, "I don't suppose we could make a deal. This bag's filled with money."

"No, I think I'll just pry it from your cold, dead hands."

"Yeah, I figured you'd say something like that." He winced. "Are you going to shoot me one limb at a time?"

"Not if you tell me what I want to know."

"Oh?" He closed his eyes and clenched his jaw. She had to give him credit; he was tougher than she'd first thought.

"Oh yes," Esme told him. "If I believe you, I'll just put one shot in the back of your head like I did to Walsh and it'll be over fast. No suffering."

"Lucky me," he gasped.

"It can be worse, Hank. It can be much worse." She knelt, cutter still aimed at him. "So what's on the chips?"

49

Cutter drawn, Bear eased up to the open door and peered inside. The blasts had stopped. He saw two cops down.

Two voices echoed from the back. Bear reasoned that during the firefight Mobley had tried to reach the tunnel. Needless to say, he hadn't made it.

He entered the building, walking softly.

The couple had their backs to him. Mobley down. The woman leaning over him. Had Bear not known any better, he'd have thought they were talking about everyday business, their tone cool and reasonable.

I don't suppose we could make a deal. This bag's filled with money.

No, I think I'll just pry it from your cold, dead hands.

Yeah, I figured you'd say something like that . . .

Bear crept closer. The woman must've followed the cops. Had she known where Mobley was earlier, it would've been a bloodbath in hookerland.

He glanced left. The subordinate cop was dead. To his right, Bear wasn't sure about the veteran. He lay motionless, but his eyes were closed rather than staring blankly into the ethers. Quite likely still alive.

The woman knelt.

So what's on the chips?

Bear waited.

"Nothing that'll keep you reading late at night," the man responded.

Esme let out a short laugh and shot him behind the right knee. Mobley screamed and rolled onto his back.

She leaned toward his ear. "Do I need to repeat myself?"

Bear didn't believe she meant repeating the question. He took careful aim. "That's enough, love."

Esme tensed.

"Drop your cutter."

Rather than obey, she pressed the end of her weapon against Mobley's forehead. "I will kill him."

"That's been your intent all along."

Mobley had finally released the satchel. Both of his hands clasped his wounded knee. "Bear," he pleaded.

"Bear?" the woman repeated. "You wouldn't be the Robin Hood of the southwest, would you?"

"I'm afraid I don't know what you're talking about." He stepped forward.

"Of course you don't," she said slowly. "And I advise you not to get any closer."

Her back was mostly to him, but his shadow loomed over them both. She was cobra cool, he thought, but unlikely to make the first move; it would be a death sentence. On the flipside of this Mexican standoff, it would take a divine stroke of luck to kill her before she squeezed the trigger. Of course, he didn't need Mobley, only the information, the transport he'd already acquired, and any cash the man had gathered.

"I sense you appraising the situation," she said.

"It doesn't look good for you, love."

"I can only imagine how it looks for him, then," she replied, pressing the cutter into the groaning man's head. "And stop calling me love."

"Merely a habit."

"Let's cut to the chase," she said. "A man like you is in it for the money. I'm guessing it's in that bag. Take it and leave. I have no quarrel with you today."

Bear gave it some thought. After all, he'd come back to the city for Father Bartholomew, not Hank Mobley. And who knew how much of what Mobley said was true, how good his information was? "It's tempting, love," he finally said.

"Stop calling me love."

"However, I made a bargain, and as ridiculous as it sounds, in the end a man's only as good as his word."

"Fools like you with their ancient creeds," she said with disgust. "Even two hundred years ago people didn't really believe that."

"I beg to differ."

"Then I'll kill him, and you'll kill me, but he'll still be dead."

"So will you," Bear pointed out.

"I'm not afraid to die."

"I know. And you'll have fulfilled your duty, correct? I guess that makes us both fools."

"If not for the circumstances, I could almost like you."

"Right up to the point you put a blast in the back of my head," he said.

"I don't think you'd be that easy."

Bear heard stirring behind him. He guessed he'd been right. The old cop wasn't dead. Depending on his condition, this complicated an already complicated situation. He didn't dare take his eyes off the woman.

"Even if he can think and see straight," she told Bear, "it'll take him a few minutes to find his cutter. So what do you say? I kill Mobley. You take the money. We both kill the cop and then go our separate ways."

"What about the computer chips?"

"You get the money," she repeated.

Bear sighed. There was no other way. "Sorry Mobley," he muttered.

He was about to shoot the woman when the rain of blasts fell toward them. No police warning. No demand they drop their weapons. Simply a series of wild blasts that flew at them from the other side of the warehouse.

Bear ducked but still didn't look back. The old man must've found the young cop's cutter, he thought.

The dark haired woman shot Mobley, taking off a portion of his head. Then with surprising agility, she pivoted toward Bear while throwing her weight to her left. In the process her cutter reeled right at him. He fired two quick blasts, and her momentum carried her dead to the ground.

"Pity," he said. "And I never even caught your name, love."

The rapid cuts continued from across the warehouse. Bear hunched, figuring that sooner or later the twisted sister of providence would cause one to strike him. He grabbed the satchel but couldn't spot the pack of computer chips he'd heard them talking about. When one blast buzzed his ear, he returned volley, half-aiming over his shoulder, knowing the shots were a token defense.

Then it stopped.

"Officer down," the old cop said in a weak voice. In the sudden stillness in the cavernous interior, Bear clearly heard the call for backup. The grizzled vet gave the address. In seconds the place would be swarming with police. Bear gave up searching for the chips and hurried toward the tunnel.

The firing commenced again.

Bear closed and secured the hatch. Then he holstered his cutter, kicked into high gear and hustled back to the never-to-be finished Vietnamese restaurant. He was up into the kitchen and out the doors with his speeder as the distant sirens grew louder. He loaded the speeder into the cargo area of the hovercraft, dropped the satchel next to it, and fired up the engine. Once he was free of the commercial center, he slowed to a putter, fitting into a stream of traffic that rubbernecked at the emergency craft speeding by.

Shame about the information, Bear thought. Then again, the veteran cop would find it, and he didn't strike Bear as anyone's dancing monkey. It could set off a political firestorm yet. Some consolation for Mobley. Then he pushed the hooligan out of his mind.

There was a reasonable chance the old cop could identify him.

It was time to get out of the city and not return for a good, long while.

50

Holland had retrieved Clute's cutter, squinted, and fired. He'd known he'd had a better chance of threading a camel through a needle's eye than striking his target, despite how large it was. Blurred vision, woozy, he went at it ancient west shotgun style, spraying as many rounds as he could with the hopes of hitting something. Someone.

He saw the man on the ground—most likely Mobley, he reasoned instinctively—die by the hand of the woman, and the woman in turn cut down by the big man. That's when Holland had called for backup.

He resumed his fire, but the big man vanished.

Impossible.

Holland stumbled toward the dead, convinced the man had found some nook to hide in. He made it halfway then fell to a knee. Blood oozed between the fingers of his right hand. He pressed it harder against his side as he let out a perverse laugh. Just now did he realized he'd been shooting left-handed. No wonder he couldn't hit anything.

It was hard to breath. He forced himself up and made it a few more steps before his legs buckled again. This time he landed on both knees and dropped on his side. He struggled to remain conscious in case the big man emerged to finish him off. But he didn't. Holland didn't hear or see anyone until the first responders arrived.

"We've got a live one," he heard a woman say as she gently rolled him onto his back. "Badly hurt." He felt her take the cutter from his hand.

"Back there," he tried to say, his voice a choked whisper. "A big man . . . computer chips . . . vital infor . . ."

"Easy, sir," she replied. "We'll get you to the hospital in no time."

Holland faded in and out as the flurry of activity picked up. The paramedics appeared and started tending his wound. Then he felt himself being strapped to a gurney. One of the last things he heard as they wheeled him into the ambulance was the order from whoever took command.

"All right ladies and gentleman, let's sweep this place. I want it so clean Lew Walsh would be proud."

51

"Mobley's dead."

"You sound disappointed."

"It came at a high price," Rex Fielder said into the vid.

"All revolutions require sacrifice. What about any compromising information?"

Fielder controlled his anger. "In our possession, senator."

"Very good. General."

52

Bear didn't see the soldiers until it was too late.

Two soldiers with rapid-fire cutters appeared behind him. Another had opened the door to the rickety bordello.

Rachel stood by sheepishly. "Sorry," she said. "They got here just before you."

Bear inched his hand down toward his cutter. The odds weren't quite in his favor, as they'd been at the warehouse. Then he spotted the young woman in robes speaking with a junior officer. They were in the hall. She turned to Bear and pointed at him. The officer approached.

Eyebrows furrowed, he asked, "Are you the driver?" He was fit as a one-handed push-up with a weather-beaten face that in a past life would've belonged to a cowboy. Or a cattle rustler, Bear speculated.

The woman in robes caught his eyes and nodded ever so slightly.

"I believe I am," Bear replied.

"I'm Lieutenant Lacewell. I have direct orders to escort you and your party out of the city."

It was Bear's turn to be wary. "To where?"

"Wherever's your destination."

"Incredible," Bear stated.

"Indeed." The lieutenant scanned the area, and with a hint of ironic wonder in his tone he declared, "It seems someone in this, ah, establishment is mighty important. The orders come from General Sam himself."

America Unbalanced

"I'm as amazed as you are," Bear told Lacewell.

"What do you care? You're just the driver." The lieutenant stepped out onto the scrap of porch. "Is that your craft?"

"A beauty, isn't it?"

"Certainly doesn't go with the neighborhood. Although I suspect someday it will." He clapped his hands. "OK, Mr. Transport Driver, gather your passengers. We have a stop to make before we leave the city limits."

Bear narrowed his eyes. If it seemed too good to be true, blast it, he reflected. Yet he bought time and uttered, "Oh?"

"Don't worry. It's a distribution center not a detention center. Someone with deep pockets is loading your little pilgrimage with a generous amount of supplies." He put up a hand. "Don't ask who. General Sam only said it was an anonymous donation. Who knows? Maybe Robin Hood struck again." He laughed as if he'd told a joke.

"Robin Hood?" Bear asked.

Lacewell shrugged. "Hey, Mother Mary might know who anonymous is since she was the one I was told to contact, but I don't have a clue and, frankly, I don't care. Now let's get it together. I'm afraid I'm going to catch something just breathing the air in this house."

"Righty-O," Bear replied.

The lieutenant strolled away.

An anonymous donation? Bear wondered. Robin Hood? He'd almost laughed alongside Lacewell. But Mother Mary?

The young woman in robes.

Marvelous, marvelous . . . so who in bloody hell is she?

53

"Good afternoon, this is Renee Short with a GNN update. At a campaign rally in Phoenix, today, Senator Leonard Litz accused President Webster of using his position to influence the outcome of the upcoming presidential election. While providing no evidence to support his charges, the Nationalist Party candidate claimed that after the Nationalist Convention in July the president ordered the FBI to spy on him and leak damaging information to undermine his candidacy. GNN reached out to the FBI but has not received a response. Here's the senator speaking."

"Weak Webster is getting desperate. He's ordered the intelligence community, in particular the Federal Bureau of Investigation, to spy on me in hopes of digging up dirt in order to influence the election. It's despicable. And it's cowardly. All I can say is keep digging, Mr. President. Go ahead. If that's how you want to spend your time instead of helping the millions of needy Americans, dig all you want. But you're only digging your own political grave because you won't find a thing."

"Press Secretary Brian Shields immediately denied the allegations, calling them preposterous. And Senator Terry Westerly, a leading critic of Litz, countered that the NP candidate was, 'making things up to draw attention from his own political woes,' a reference to the ongoing calls for an investigation of the awarding of federal contracts for the southwest desalination project. Until recently the project had been shut down but signs lately indicate it may have found a new life.

"At the same rally, Senator Litz also came to the defense of Isabelle Bishop, wife of vice presidential candidate J. Henry Bishop, calling her 'one of the best women he knows' and dismissing unconfirmed reports as lies that, when still a teenager, she'd had an abortion in Mexico. 'It's bad enough

149

they make things up about me,' he said, 'but this goes too far.' The Bishop campaign offered no comment.

"This is Renee Short with GNN. Have a good day."

54

Bear didn't breath easy until his military guardians were on their way back to the city. Even so, he had to admit that at one point they'd been worth their weight in cutters.

At a newly constructed checkpoint right before they reached the Barrens, Bear had been ordered out of the hovercraft. Lieutenant Lacewell, who'd occupied the seat next to him, intervened.

"These people are with us, Sergeant."

"Sorry, sir, but the driver meets the description of a suspect wanted for questioning in a double homicide."

"This man's been with me. Let us pass."

"I have my orders, sir. They come straight from Colonel Fielder."

"Tell Colonel Fielder to blow it out his ass."

For a second the sergeant was speechless. "Are you refusing to follow orders, sir?"

"Not in the least, sonny boy. My orders come straight from General Samuel T. Leatherwood, and I'm about as loyal to General Sam as a man can get. Now you're going to let us pass, or I'm going to stomp on your eyelids. And then I'll have you busted back to private. Do you understand?"

The sergeant stiffened and trembled a little as he saluted. "Yes, sir."

After they'd cleared the checkpoint, Bear said, "You were rather hard on the sergeant. He was really not much more than a boy."

"I don't have patience for non-coms trying to order me around."

"I see. And who is Colonel Fielder?"

For once Lacewell fell silent before responding, "No one you want to know."

"Why's that?"

"He's a mean son-of-a-bitch, and if General Sam didn't have my back, I might've turned you over to that kid."

"Marvelous."

"Exactly. Let me give you a piece of advice, my friend. Whatever it is you do—and I'm sure you're an upstanding citizen—stay clear of Fielder." Lacewell then had crossed his arms, closed his eyes, and leaned back in his seat, effectively ending the conversation.

"Good to know," Bear had muttered.

"What's good to know?" Father Bartholomew now asked, bringing Bear back to the present. He'd not realized he'd spoken aloud.

"It'd be good to know where Xavier and Francis have gotten off to," he said. Bear had stopped at a small outpost nestled in a patch of white pine, spruce and fir trees, tough evergreens that hung on against the blistering sun. Soon the landscape would shift to flatlands of sage with clusters of mesquite and scrub oak, scars of the old highway system poking through every so often along with shells of abandoned buildings and the rubble of lost horizons.

"How are we going to do that?" Bartholomew asked.

"There's a chap out here who's opened a pub," Bear explained.

"A pub?"

"Believe me, if Litz is elected it'll do wonders for the alcohol industry. At any rate, the pub's not much to look at, not yet anyway, but if anyone knows the comings and goings around here, it's Graham Bly, its owner, bartender, and, I might add, accomplished brew master."

The last scrap of information struck a spark in Bartholomew's eyes. "Accomplished brew master? By all means, let's go see Mr. Bly. But what about the others?"

"Tell them to stretch their legs and explore some of the shops." That would probably take all of ten minutes, but he'd leave that for them to discover.

"I'll let them know. Did you know that once upon a time there used to be a play land of sorts for adults out here? An homage to the renaissance, if you can believe that. Some college professors were excavating the festival site, but sadly the money ran dry, like it and the water has everywhere."

Bear drew in a deep breath as he waited. The hot air smelled of pine.

Clean and fresh, he thought. Whether or not that was true didn't matter. Just that it felt that way compared to the city gave him a sense of relief.

Lieutenant Lacewell had thought this was their final destination. Bear didn't correct him out of fear they'd be saddled with the soldiers as they ventured out into the Wasteland. The added firepower wasn't worth the risk of Lacewell deciding they were all fools and forcing them back to what he considered civilization. The soldiers had served their purpose. It'd been time to cut them free.

Bartholomew returned. The young woman in robes was with him. Bear wondered if she favored accomplished brew masters, too.

They fell in step. "What's your name?" Bear asked her.

"Sister Maria Ashley."

"And before you were Sister Maria Ashley, who were you?'

"No one special."

Bartholomew started to speak but Bear raised his hand, silencing him. "No one special?" he asked. "Yet you invited an armed escort."

"Why do you think the escort was for me?"

Bear didn't dignify that with an answer.

"You'll soon learn that Bear has uncanny insight," Bartholomew spoke up. "Very little gets by him."

Maria Ashley scowled. "Believe me, that was more for another's convenience than for mine."

Bear waited.

"Very well. My sister is married to a powerful politician." She paused then added, "He may also be the next vice president of the United States. I can only hope you'll keep this to yourself. I'm no longer close to my sister, and I suspect her help was so she could be rid of me. My calling is an embarrassment to her."

"Did you know this?" Bear asked Bartholomew.

The priest nodded. "She told me the night she came to us."

"I'll keep it to myself, and I advise you to do the same," Bear told them. "There are some disreputable people out here who'd welcome that information."

"I only told you because I trust you," Maria Ashley said.

"Well, be careful about trusting people, too. I'm aware that's not in your job description, but you're no longer in your typical workplace." Bear stopped in front of a modest cabin where a hanging sign simple read *Graham's Pub*. "Ah, here we are. It's a bit small, but there's room to expand."

The interior was rustic—wooden floors, a dozen or so tables and mismatched chairs—and behind the makeshift bar stood a large man smoking a pipe and reading a book. He had salt and pepper hair, a wide clean-shaven face, and he looked up and smiled when he noticed them. "Ah, Bear, good to see you." He waved the book. "Do you know a shop opened that actually sells these ancient artifacts? Cheap, too. Of course, that's because people don't read anymore. And when an electorate stops reading, they can be sheared like sheep and led to the slaughter." He winked. "As we've seen."

"Hello, Graham. I didn't come to talk treason today. Three pints of your special."

The bartender set his pipe in an ashtray and poured out three draughts. Bear, Bartholomew and Maria Ashley took stools at the bar.

"Go slow," Bear warned his two mates. "This isn't city beer. It has a kick."

Graham relit his pipe. "Odd traveling companions," he commented.

"We're looking for a couple of Brothers."

"Xavier and Francis," said the bartender. "Makes sense."

Bear nodded as he gulped his drink. He sighed. If there was anything more satisfying than the piney air, it was a good stout.

"They went north," Graham added. "Rumor has it that on the far side of the New Salt Basin there's a patch of an Oasis. Mind you it's just rumor, and you have to cross hundreds of miles of desert. I guess the brothers decided it was worth the risk."

"And they went alone?"

"Somehow they managed to hire themselves a guide."

"You don't say. And who would that be?"

Graham's smile broadened. "Celeste."

"The Scrap?" Bear responded, incredulous.

"The one and only."

"How did they swing that?"

"Must be her name," the bartender stated offhandedly.

Bear took a hearty drink of his stout. "What do you mean?"

"Heavenly with the Brothers." He wiped the counter with the rag. "Did you know they intend to call their new utopia Sophia? What kind of name is that?"

"Ancient," replied Bear. "The Gnostics considered her the feminine aspect of God. Mother of wisdom. Some thought her the very soul of humankind. Or all of the above. I trust they're looking at her as the spark of the divine, the new light with which to guide themselves."

"Ask and you shall receive," Graham muttered. "Although it makes sense now why they're going to call themselves the Neo-Gnos. If they survive."

"The light of God will survive," Bear said matter-of-factly. Even if the ancient Gnostics were suspect of God and considered their beliefs more of a pathway to salvation. But beliefs change, religions and pathways adjust. Thus, he guessed, the Neo, the new, in the Gnosticism.

"You know what I mean," Graham retorted.

"I do. And I meant what I said." Bear finished his pint and shifted his attention to Bartholomew as he debated on a second. "Sure you won't burst into flames if you take up with this new cult?"

"Christianity began as a cult, too."

"But a good Catholic boy like you?"

"If anything I'm like our response to the climate—adaptable."

"That speaks volumes of our times. Indeed volumes on many levels." Bear grinned at Maria Ashley, impressed she'd finished her pint. Father Bartholomew had half remanding. "And what about you?" he asked her.

"I favor Eastern mysticism. I don't think it'll be a problem." She ran a finger around the rim of her empty glass. "Where do you stand on the subject of religion?"

"On my own two feet, love," he replied.

"That's no answer," she challenged.

"Quite true. And I'll not insult you with my Church of England rhetoric. Suffice it to say my history is long and complicated. Perhaps someday when we have time for a second pint I'll regale you with it. Perhaps by then it'll also mean more to you than if I told you now.

"Bottoms up, Padre," the big man added. "Looks like we have miles and miles to go before we sleep."

55

After journeying through a lunar-like landscape, the appearance of trees in the distance was jarring. They'd crossed Texas and turned north at the Yellow Ruins and continued a far stretch.

An Amarillo road sign lay half-buried in the sand, as did one for Tucumcari, a ghost town they'd have hit had they continued west.

Bear now rubbed his eyes, wondering if he'd manifested the image out of desperate boredom. A good old-fashion mirage. The closer he drew, though, the more real it became. A vision of hope? He wasn't sure about that. At least it wasn't heat waves playing tricks.

"Glory be," Father Bartholomew uttered.

Yet there were occasional flashes of cutter fire, and that disturbed him. He knew he'd been spotted leagues away so no matter how cautiously he approached, they saw he was coming. Not until he crossed into the camp did he realize the flashes had belonged to Celeste. She'd been hunting wild dogs. Pelts were stretched out everywhere.

The hovercraft attracted a fair amount of attention from the handful of souls in the fledgling garden of Sophia. Bear introduced Bartholomew and Maria Ashley to Xavier and Francis. Francis was particularly attentive to them. Bear stepped away, leaving them to get acquainted.

"These tenderfeet don't understand what living off the land means," Celeste told Bear as he approached her. Even though he'd powered a large hovercraft into their primitive compound, she hadn't budged from her work.

"Naturally. On the other hand, one could accuse you of going tribal."

"What are you doing here?" she asked as she scraped the fat off a hide.

"I could ask a nice girl like you the same thing."

"I told you before I'm not a nice girl," she reminded him.

After scanning the area, Bear grinned. "I might not believe you this time." Lean-tos were nestled within the cluster of cypress and live oak trees. Close by the gurgle of water fascinated him, a sound virtually unheard of in these parts. Most riverbeds had gone bone dry, whatever water that was left sliding deep underground. Bear found it amazing no one else had claimed this spot. He could already hear Brother Francis pronounce it sacred ground saved by divine providence for them.

"The pay was right," she added, "and I wanted to scout the territory. Besides, these rookies crossed paths with the wrong men back on the Rim. Lucky for the rooks, I didn't like the dudes and discouraged their aggression."

"I can only imagine. As for me, I brought more rooks for the roost."

Actually, only half of the passengers he'd driven out of the city had made the final leg of the trip. Even Carlos and Gabe, Father Bartholomew's church workers, had opted to stay with their families at the settlement on the Rim. They'd responded to a help wanted sign at a newly built recycling center and been hired on the spot. A wise move, Bear thought. With resources dwindling, recycling was bound to grow beyond what anyone had originally predicted. In fact, a good way to scratch out a living here was to mine old landfills for plastic and metals. Live off the excess of the past. The Scraps were quickly figuring that out.

"This has the makings of quite a set-up," Bear commented. "Seems it'd be hard for a Scrap to leave."

"Or a crazy-assed loner," Celeste shot back.

Bear chuckled. "Fair enough. But I can see where it'll be hard to defend."

"As the old book says, the supreme dude giveth, and the same all mighty supreme dude taketh away." She paused her work and added, "That's why I don't trust men."

"I'm hurt."

"I couldn't hurt you with a blaster." She resumed scraping the hide.

"Perhaps it wouldn't be taken away if someone was willing to help."

Again Celeste stopped working on the hide she was tanning. "I'm catching some disturbing vibes from you."

"You're a warrior trapped in a scavenger's skin. You could train them."

She stared at him as if mushrooms had started sprouting out of his ears. "Who? The dynamic duo of Xavier and Francis? Or maybe you mean the spindly priest you just transported here. Your noodle's been baking in the

157

sun way too long, my large misguided friend."

"Friend? I thought you didn't like men."

"You're growing on me."

"Well, you're right. Xavier and Bartholomew aren't warrior-priests by any means. But don't underestimate Francis. He may appear slow, but he has a survivor's will. And look around. There are a number of young possibilities."

"Maybe three," she replied without looking up. "At the outside, four. So knock yourself out and train them to your heart's content."

"I'm not seeking a job."

He'd caught her off-guard.

"Who says I am?"

"You haven't left," he pointed out. "Not only that but—"

"I know," she interrupted. "I've gone tribal." She stood, blade in hand. "I might not look it, but I'm too young to play wet nurse to desert bait."

"Pity. You have much to offer them. And yourself."

"Your lame psychology won't work on me," she told him.

"Of course not." Bear faced the direction from which he'd come. "I suspect they'll want this to be an open, welcoming place, God help them. But they'll need a watch list in order to rotate sentry duty. And don't you think they could use some kind of barrier over there? At least to keep the wild dogs at bay."

"Sure, no problem. Why don't you snap your fingers, magic man? I'm sure a fine fence will appear."

Bear grinned. "You'll be amazed at the supplies the army donated."

It seemed for the first time Celeste took in the magnitude of the hovercraft he'd powered. "You don't intend to leave that machine, do you? They'll just get it stolen."

"Not with you around, love."

And he walked off, leaving her to mutter and curse to herself. He intended to inventory the satchel of money. All the girl needed now was a little incentive. Some to catch her interest with the promise of more later. That ought to tip the scale.

Maybe then they'd have a fighting chance.

Epilogue

The Post Election Paradise Blues

56

"My fellow Americans," Leonard Litz said, "I am humbled by your confidence in me, by your faith in me, and I am proud to be your next president. Together we will do great things. I promise. America will be beautiful again . . . "

Holland turned the big screen off before it ruined his appetite.

Weeks had passed since the inauguration and GNN still played snippets of Litz's speech as if it was the greatest compilation of words since MLK's I have a dream. In reality it was fast-food propaganda feeding junk to starving people. People who didn't even show up for the inauguration; smallest crowd in history. Yet, some fools were eating it up.

Speaking of fools, it appeared there were many Lew Walshes in the world. Whatever information Mobley had possessed had disappeared with his soul. True to his word, the investigating officer had mopped the warehouse clean, bleaching any hint of justice from the crime report. When Holland had asked where the computer chips were, he received a series of blank stares. He persisted, making a general nuisance of himself, until finally the deputy commissioner told him that if—and that was a big *if*— such evidence existed, then the man who got away must've taken it.

He didn't buy it. Had the big man retained the information, Holland had a strong feeling it would've been all over the media, both mainstream and underground. Why else would they have risked coming back to the warehouse? It couldn't have been just for money. Besides, Mobley was willing to trade the chips for his freedom, saying his partner would approve. That right there was indication they meant to leak it.

I bet with a little police work, you'll get your justice. It might even make you chief.

How wrong that poor bastard had been.

And to rub salt into the wound, Lew's card with Skyler's number written on the back was also missing. Holland hadn't realized it until he'd searched his wallet during the deputy commissioner's visit. Everything else was there—license, vid-credit chips, a couple of tens—but the business card was gone. At some point someone had lifted it from him.

Holland couldn't believe it. Any of it; or, sadly, he could.

And now Litz had actually won.

"That man will sponge every word from the tombstones of our past he doesn't agree with," he said to the chicken he was basting. There were potatoes and carrots as well, fresh from his hothouse. It was supposed to be a celebration dinner. Instead it felt more like food a neighbor would drop off during a time of mourning.

The gate com chimed. Leaning on a cane, Holland went to the front window and saw Bernie, Kelly, and the baby right on time. He buzzed them in.

"Well, how's the little man?" Holland asked once they'd settled inside.

"Doctor says he's strong as an bull," Kelly replied.

"Given his parents, that doesn't surprise me one bit." Despite the heat, Kelly had him wrapped in a lightweight blanket. Holland brushed a corner of it from the baby's face and looked at him. "So what's his name?"

"Joseph Kirkland Hawke," Bernie said. "Joseph after my father, and Kirkland is Kelly's maiden name."

Holland knew that, of course, but he just nodded. They'd wanted to add Holland to the mix—Joseph Kirkland Holland Hawke—but he'd talked them out of it. "The poor kid doesn't need a name as long as the seventh Earl of Essex, or some fool thing," he'd argued.

"Want to hold him?" Kelly asked.

"Maybe later when I'm sitting down." He tapped the cane against the floor. "I'm still a bit rickety when upright."

"Smells good in here," Bernie observed.

"Well, make yourselves at home. Bernie, there's beer in the icebox. Pop a couple open. Kelly?"

She shook her head. "Not now, though I might indulge in one with dinner." She settled in a chair in the living room, the baby awake and making an occasional squeak and coo. "So, how's retirement, Holland?"

"Harder than I thought it'd be." He accepted a beer from Bernie and sat on the couch. "There's a lot going on out there, most of it not good, and I'm stuck watching it on that fool thing"—he motioned to the dark vid screen—"like an old man in a nursing home."

Kelly frowned.

"But I don't want to get into that," Holland quickly amended. After all, they'd gone over and over what had happened in the warehouse until there was really nothing left to say. Bernie had even tried to continue the investigation only to be stonewalled, and then abruptly he was transferred to his new position. "So how's the new job?" he asked.

"You're right, Skip Gallagher's a good guy. He's not you, but he'll do."

Holland chuckled. "That's probably in his favor."

"But you called it," Bernie added. "Things are fixing to change fast."

"They already have."

"No, even more. They're going to bubble the city with those electromagnetic shields the government's been developing. They call it climate adaptability."

"How the heck do they expect to pay for that?"

"They've tightened the borders even more. If anyone wants to get in now, word has it they'll have to pay a citizenship fee, the proceeds of which will go directly to the bubble fund."

"They won't let enough people in to pay for beans," Holland complained.

"They also figure with so many people unemployed they have a huge pool of cheap labor, especially if they keep out the workers from south of the border."

"So we're going isolationist."

"We've been heading that way for a long time, Holland," Kelly spoke up. "This is just the nail in the global coffin."

Bernie glanced at Kelly as if he had more bad news to deliver.

"Well, what else?" Holland asked.

"Tell him," she prompted.

"The bubble won't come this far out. I've seen the plans and it looks, with exception of protecting the desalination plant, they'll cover the city proper only—"

"And gentrify it," Holland cut in.

"Of course," Kelly said.

Bernie sighed. "You'll be part of the Rim," he added.

Holland grinned. "Goddamn, that's the best news I've heard in a dog's day."

The young couple reacted with surprise. "I thought you'd be pissed off," Bernie said.

"Hell no," the former cop replied. "I don't want to be part of their Shangri-La. Now I've got something to celebrate. Let's eat!"

57

Isabelle Bishop listened.

Concerned, she lightly drummed her fingernails against the side of her teacup. They sat across from each other at breakfast at Number One Observatory Circle, the official residency for the vice president. She'd not seen J. Henry this agitated since Robert the gardener had left the water on and flooded the tomato plants in the hothouse.

"I thought the idea of turning the New Dust Bowl into a prison was political nonsense that came from the other side."

"They call it the Wasteland, and I think if it was up to Litz, he'd send all of what's left of the independent press there." He tried to smile as if he'd told a joke then said, "Not only that, there's talk of lifting the term limit on the presidency," he told her.

"Already?"

"A lot of talk. Wait. You expected it?"

"It was a very emotional election. Why would the aftermath be any less emotional or controversial?"

J. Henry grunted and poked at his eggs with his fork.

"Oh, darling, if there's one thing I've learned in my political infancy is that this town is full of talk. Action doesn't necessarily follow."

"We're entering a new era. I expect to see more executive orders and unilateral moves than ever before."

"Even President Litz can't by-pass congress."

"The man knows how to play the system. I wouldn't be surprised if he tries to get congress to vote itself out of existence."

"You sound as if you're having second thoughts. Darling, you're the number two person in the country."

"In what John Adams called the most insignificant office that ever the invention of man contrived. Don't mistake my apprehension for disloyalty. I'm completely in the president's corner. I just don't plan to spend the rest of my career playing hatchet man and attending PR events. I'll go back to congress first."

"Well, I believe you'll get your chance at the number one job."

"Not if Litz is in it for life." He put down his fork. "And I'm beginning to believe that's his intention."

"That was never part of the deal."

"Welcome to D.C., my dear, where deal or not everyone has his own agenda."

58

One evening Francis joined Bear as the sinking sun syphoned the sandy light from another brittle day. Not far from where they stood, Celeste had three young men and one young woman out on the makeshift cutter range. She was teaching them how to shoot.

"You made your choice," Francis said with a crooked smile.

Bear shook his head. "No, I'm still a weapons runner."

"Are you?"

"This was a one time shot. I did what I had to do, mate."

"Yes, the right thing. Your mother would be proud."

What an odd comment, he thought. From anyone else, he would've taken it as a conversational go-to, but something about Francis in his short history of knowing him told Bear he spoke when he had something to say and was hardly prone to small talk.

"Perhaps she would," he replied safely. "She spent half her life trying to help me understand right from wrong."

"A remarkable woman."

Bear grew wary. "You couldn't possibly have known my mum."

"Not in this life, very true."

"You must be an old soul indeed," Bear stated a little more flippantly than he'd intended.

Brother Francis tugged on his lower lip, untouched by the gentle taunt. "We all have much to learn. Remember you're welcome here anytime," he added. Then in his typical absentminded fashion, he wandered away without another word.

Remarkable woman? Bear echoed. If Francis only knew.

Or perhaps somehow he did.

Celeste and her recruits had called it a day. Bear paced to the fringe of the camp and watched the last of the sun fade. He couldn't help but feel the moment was like a false spring, a flash of January warmth before the cold of winter once again set in. Of course, few besides Bear recalled either, and he wasn't one to long for the past, but in the current climate—both literally and politically—a touch of yearning seemed appropriate.

This spark of hope that surrounded him faced an overwhelming darkness. Fortunately for them, they had a light maiden to help them get their feet on the ground. She didn't know who she was, not yet, anyway. Soon, though, she would, and any light against the darkness was welcomed.

Yes, any light. He sighed. Life was looking so much easier when he was just a weapon's runner.

Bear turned back to the fires in the camp, wood being much too sparse to simply burn at random anymore. He saw full bellies and temporary contentedness. Let them enjoy the moment, he thought. We're all in for a rough ride.

Night fell. A chill went through him in spite of the heat. *A rabbit just jumped over your grave*, his old mum would've said. They'll be many chills in the years to come, he thought. Many chills before the true light returns.

Before a new generation rises against the dark.

It's now a world where a single drop of water is more precious than gold. President Litz is dead; The Water Cartel is in power, Bear, Bernie and now Joey continue the fight, joined by an unlikely group of survivors. . . read on to discover the next part of the story—

The
Wastelanders

Tim Hemlin

1

The explosion rocked the Houston Bubble from the port to the western suburbs in Sugar Land. One witness said a plume of flames shot so high it could've burned God in the ass. An ocean of smoke rolled across the self-contained sky. Cartel officials reconfigured the energy walls quickly, yet everyone within its protective maze smelled the acrid, deathlike odor— everyone was subject to high levels of radiation. Concrete lay split open like broken egg shells. Metal and cables twisted and protruded as if a massacre of machine warriors had taken place on the moon.

One hundred and sixty-five people died in the blast at the desalination plant. The workday had just begun. Of the scanty remains, only fragments were fit to be scanned for DNA identification. Amongst the concrete rubble and the melted wires and the smoldering infirmed metal, bone meal baked beneath the brittle sun.

The reason Bernie Hawke wasn't number one sixty-six was due to a case of food poisoning. He'd eaten alone the night before at Sweet Chop Stix, a retro twentieth century Chinese buffet, and as far as he could tell a bad piece of chicken flattened him. Uncle Al, the owner of the buffet and an old friend, apologized profusely when Bernie, sweaty and sick, his intestines in a bind, called him the next morning. Uncle Al blamed the supplier. Bernie suspected Al's sloppy son-in-law cook, Chen, as the fat slob liked to nip at the bottle while working.

Because he wasn't victim one sixty-six, the authorities came for him at his floating apartment complex almost immediately. The Cartel's data base kept national, not just local, records of their employee's activities. A bulldog sergeant explained that it was routine procedure—they were rounding up all the people who hadn't been at Cartel #23 earlier. Mostly the police and feds were interviewing the night staff—cleaning crews and security and the few techs needed to maintain the desalination plant. Yet they were also highly interested in the handful who should've been at work but weren't.

"You can talk to Uncle Al at Sweet Chop Stix," Bernie told a Home Sec agent. He was a rod-up-your-ass young guy by the name of Crisp. Fit, chiseled, Agent Crisp was the type who did push-ups even while making love.

"Aye, we did, lad."

Bernie looked at Crisp's partner. He was, like Bernie, an older heavy-set guy, the kind who lumbered a little as he walked. His name was O'Hare. As was the fashion these days among some ethnicities, O'Hare peppered his speech patterns with a touch of the ancient accent. In his case, of course, the Irish brogue.

He sat in the stark windowless room. Surveillance devices captured his every move. As he rested his elbows on the stainless steel table, the interrogation brought to his mind movies he'd seen depicting New York and Chicago a couple of hundred years ago—perhaps in a past life O'Hare had battled Al Capone. Someone, Bernie thought, should be smoking even though smoking was outlawed within the Bubble. The light was harsh. The room was stuffy. And in the corner rested the lie scanner.

Yet Bernie liked O'Hare as, naturally, he was supposed to. Complimenting his dark eyes and graying black hair O'Hare wore a folksy smile—the good one in this good-cop, bad-cop duo.

"And?" asked Bernie.

"And he said that you called him around ten o'clock last night but that he hadn't heard any other such complaints."

"People like to complain," Crisp added. "People like to sue. It's easy money."

"You can check out my water bill," said Bernie. "You'll notice a rather large rise in activity the past few hours."

"Don't be a wise-ass."

O'Hare raised his hand. "Now, now, lad, Deputy Hawke deserves to be treated with respect." He smiled as though he and Bernie were best of friends. "You're feeling better, I see."

"My stomach's begun to settle."

"Good, good. Yes, lad," he addressed Crisp, "if Deputy Hawke says that he was ill then the law suggests we take him at his word. For the time being."

"I say hook him up to the scanner."

"Now, we're all men of the law. I believe in my heart that we can talk as professionals. Isn't that so, Deputy Hawke?"

Bernie didn't like the way this was going. "GNN is calling the explosion an act of terrorism." Of course, the Government News Network would be quick to call it an act of terrorism as the current administration fed its power by drawing the blood of fear from the masses like a vampire.

"Aye, lad, it was sabotage. The force of the discharge alone ruled out faulty equipment and human error, never mind the bump in radiation."

"A burner?" Bernie, calm, laced his thick hands together, his square clean-shaven face impassive—yet the use of limited atomics set off a number of alarms, the loudest of which demanding to know how the Bubble's tight security had been breached.

"Apparently so."

"Has anyone claimed responsibility?"

"Not as of yet."

"Unusual," muttered Bernie.

"Aye," agreed O'Hare. "Very unusual. The scum which does this sort of disgusting thing normally wants the world to know its name."

"You have any suspects?"

"That's what we're working on, my boy."

"We ask the questions," inserted Crisp. Crisp, as Bernie talked, had strangely grown more and more tense.

"You're thinking it was a Wastelander," Bernie said, though he wasn't quite sure why, initially, those words came from his mouth.

"Now what would you be knowing about Wastelanders?"

A peculiar, twisted smile touched Crisp's thin lips. Yes, Bernie thought, that was it. Of course they'd know.

"Enough that I don't want to be one," replied Bernie.

"You're damn right you don't want to be one," Crisp stated and leaned close. "Exposed all day to brutal heat, to the blistering sun, to skin-singeing ozone—"

"I know, not to mention the packs of wild dogs, blah, blah, blah."

Crisp's face went crimson.

Bernie's knowledge of the Wasteland went beyond the propaganda shown on GNN. Everyone knew that once the climate changed in the way scientists had been predicting since the mid-twentieth century, the U.S. breadbasket went stale. It dried up due to drought. Topsoil blew like crumbs. Bernie had made a study of the area. True, the American midwest bore a closer resemblance to Death Valley than the sea of wheat for which it had once been famous. True, common rhetoric called the area the Wasteland, yet few people knew about the satellite photos that showed an occasional oasis. The government withheld that information to discourage thrill seekers as the oases were considered few and far between. And the scrap of humanity that lived there was depicted as barbarous, dwarfed in their evolutionary growth and akin to animals.

Yes, Bernie had made an intense study of the land beyond the Rim. He'd hardly kept it a secret. Naively, perhaps, he'd believed that if he made his actions transparent then he'd remain beyond suspicion of anti-social behavior. Apparently he'd been wrong.

"I guarded the inner border for two years," Crisp growled.

"Where, now, would Wastelanders be getting explosive devices of such magnitude?" wondered O'Hare aloud.

"They wouldn't," answered Crisp.

"And how do you suppose Wastelanders could gain access to the complex of Water Cartel #23?"

"They couldn't," Crisp again replied, "without an inside man."

Bernie put his hands up as though he could stop their thoughts. "Whoa, I'm as loyal as the next American—"

"Of course, lad, we see that you've signed your loyalty oath."

"As a deputy security officer you can get whoever you want inside," added Crisp.

"Word has it, lad, you were expected to take over as head of security once Chief Gallagher—one of my own, God rest his soul—retired."

"Skip Gallagher was a friend of mine," Bernie said. "Not just a boss."

"We're aware of that, too, lad. Our condolences."

O'Hare said the words but Bernie felt no emotion standing behind them.

Bernie was a former cop. He'd left the force to go into private practice. Too many jobs, though, of peeping at cheating husbands and wives brought him down, which was why he took the spot at Cartel #23. Getting inside the Cartel wasn't easy, but once in you were made for life. Good benefits. Good retirement package. Desalination was the name of the game, taking over the country's infrastructure the way the oil and gas industry once had.

But Bernie's instincts told him they were looking for a scapegoat, and it wasn't simply because he'd been absent from the job.

"Yes, Chief Gallagher was a family man, wasn't he?"

Bernie nodded. Here it came.

"As are you."

"I live alone," Bernie said. "My wife passed away six years ago."

"I imagine that was a difficult time, lad. But you have a son, too, yes?"

"Joey."

"Joseph Kirkland Hawke," said Crisp. "Gone missing from civilized society."

"Gone missing where, lad?"

"I don't know."

"Don't lie to us," Crisp snapped and pointedly looked toward the scanner.

"I'm not lying," Bernie calmly replied. "I was never able to find him."

O'Hare stroked his cheeks. "Come, now, Mr. Hawke, let's have it."

"We know you requested to cross the inner border," said Crisp. "You know more about the Wasteland than you're letting on."

Bernie took a deep breath. "It's true I asked to go into the Wasteland. Chief Gallagher took up for me when the request was denied. After my wife died, well, both my son and I went a little mad. I drank too much. He dropped out of society. He started hanging around the Rim with some fringe people and I'm afraid they brainwashed him. By the time I'd sobered, he was gone."

Crisp said nothing.

Bernie eyed O'Hare—a plea for understanding. "You know how bad those cults can be."

"Which cult, Deputy Hawke?"

"The Neo-Gnostics."

"'Tis true you wouldn't be the first man to lose a child to those hooligans. Yet the fact remains you never found your son, Mr. Hawke."

"I don't even know if Joey went into the Wasteland." Bernie paused. "Or if he's even still alive."

"So you've had no contact with him," said Crisp.

Bernie shook his head. "He left almost a year to the day after Kelly died. I've not seen him since."

"You're lying," repeated Crisp.

Bernie's head jerked up as though he'd hit. "What?"

"Our lads down at the station have been sifting through the video footage," O'Hare stated. "No one comes or goes in this city without us noticing."

Stunned, Bernie asked, "What are you saying?"

"I'm saying, lad, that the computer has pulled up an image of a young man."

Crisp, who'd opened a file on his vid-com, placed the device in the middle of the table. Up popped a handful of enlarged holographic images. They automatically cycled through.

Bernie stared, too dumbfounded to speak. The figure that hovered before him had long hair and he wore a beard but those eyes, those blue eyes, Kelly's eyes—there was no doubt Bernie was looking at his son, Joey.

Crisp's thin smile became downright predatory.

"Perhaps, lad, it's true you had nothing to do with the bombing," said O'Hare. "You must admit, however, it appears you might know how to help us locate the culprit."

Buy The Wastelanders on **Amazon US**, **Amazon UK** or **Amazon India**

About the Author

Tim Hemlin is a graduate of the University of New Hampshire, having studied with poets Charles Simic and Mekeel McBride. He has published in poetry journals, anthologies, and magazines—most notably in Ellery Queen. He was nominated for the PWA's prestigious Shamus award in 1998. Currently he has six novels out.

For ten years he was a chef for a high-end catering company in Houston. In 1992 he switched careers and taught middle school ELA for 22 years. Two years ago he decided to put his master's degree to work and is now a high school counselor. In addition, he is an avid marathoner, fly-fisherman, and outdoorsman. He lives just outside Houston, Texas with his wife Valerie, two dogs and a very cantankerous cat.

Visit Tim's **Online Bookstore** link page at www.TimHemlin.com

Loooking for another great dystopian read?

All of the Flesh Served

Terry M. West

Any record of the 45th that does not recognize him as a prophet is propaganda and a lie. False history. The truth is with the 45th. His word is absolute for it is God's word...

Hundreds of years after the great cataclysm, the Ministry of the 45th survive in a network of scientific bunkers. The last bastion of the old holy order, the 45th are bent on rebuilding the scorched earth and eliminating God's enemies. The Ministry wages a war against the mutant topsiders that occupy the dead states of the Soviet Union of America. Defending the 45th are the Red Guard, genetically engineered soldiers who are programmed to obey through their lifebrand. Dr. Morgan is a serviceman for Unit 468 of the Red Guard. His lifebrand being medicine, Dr. Morgan is the longest surviving field medic to serve. But Dr. Morgan is a deeply conflicted man with violent fantasies that contradict his pledge to preserve life. After escaping an abduction by the topsiders, Dr. Morgan's faith is cracked. During a furlough in the high Chancellor's bunker, Dr. Morgan is hailed a hero and taken off the front lines. But he soon realizes that someone has altered his lifebrand and lifted the veil that concealed the greatest deception ever perpetrated. Dr. Morgan has just become the most dangerous man in the wastelands. And when he discovers who the real enemy is, the revelation unleashes a fury strong enough to destroy what is left of the earth.

All of the Flesh Served is a disturbing vision of what could one day come.